S0-AZP-084

"For tonight, I'm just Zach. And you're just Jessie. No last names. No family between us."

"Can we do that?" she asked, her voice shaking with confusion while her body pulsed with desire.

"We can do anything we want." Zach pressed his mouth against the curve of her throat and she closed her eyes, arching her back to offer him greater access. "Give us tonight, Jessie."

She struggled with her conscience while the vow she'd made at ten years old to hate all Kerrigans faded beneath the force of her own desire. *He's not like the rest of them.* She fumbled behind her and twisted the doorknob, allowing the door to swing inward. She saw a flare of satisfaction in his eyes before he swung her off her feet and carried her into the apartment.

Dear Reader,

I fell in love with northeast Montana when I was five years old. That was the year my family moved there to help my great-uncle work his wheat-and-cattle ranch just north of Peerless. I saw my first real horseman when neighbor Tony Kleeman joined my father to run the Hereford cattle into the home pasture for the winter. The fluid rhythm of Tony riding a quarter horse was like watching choreographed ballet. I was wide-eyed, awed, amazed and left with an image I've never forgotten.

The ranchers who work the land in Daniels County and elsewhere in Montana are rugged, independent individuals, and the women who share their lives are equally strong. But like families everywhere, pride, prejudice, betrayal and intrigue can complicate their lives. I hope you enjoy this story about Jessie McCloud, Zach Kerrigan and their struggle to create a family for their much-loved son, Rowdy. And I hope you'll return to Wolf Creek with me for the third installment in The McClouds of Montana when Chase McCloud reluctantly joins forces with Raine Harper to search for her missing brother.

Warmest wishes,

Lois Faye Dyer

JESSIE'S CHILD

LOIS FAYE DYER

SPECIAL EDITION®

Published by Silhouette Books

America's Publisher of Contemporary Romance

If you purchased this book without a cover you should be aware
that this book is stolen property. It was reported as "unsold and
destroyed" to the publisher, and neither the author nor the
publisher has received any payment for this "stripped book."

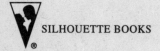 SILHOUETTE BOOKS

ISBN-13: 978-0-373-24776-9
ISBN-10:   0-373-24776-1

JESSIE'S CHILD

Copyright © 2006 by Lois Faye Dyer

All rights reserved. Except for use in any review, the reproduction
or utilization of this work in whole or in part in any form by any
electronic, mechanical or other means, now known or hereafter
invented, including xerography, photocopying and recording, or in
any information storage or retrieval system, is forbidden without
the written permission of the editorial office, Silhouette Books,
233 Broadway, New York, NY 10279 U.S.A.

All characters in this book have no existence outside the imagination of
the author and have no relation whatsoever to anyone bearing the same
name or names. They are not even distantly inspired by any individual
known or unknown to the author, and all incidents are pure invention.

This edition published by arrangement with Harlequin Books S.A.

® and TM are trademarks of Harlequin Books S.A., used under license.
Trademarks indicated with ® are registered in the United States Patent
and Trademark Office, the Canadian Trade Marks Office and in other
countries.

Visit Silhouette Books at www.eHarlequin.com

Printed in U.S.A.

Books by Lois Faye Dyer

Silhouette Special Edition

Lonesome Cowboy #1038
He's Got His Daddy's Eyes #1129
The Cowboy Takes a Wife #1198
The Only Cowboy for Caitlin #1253
Cattleman's Courtship #1306
Cattleman's Bride-To-Be #1457
Practice Makes Pregnant #1569
Cattleman's Heart #1611
The Prince's Bride #1640
Luke's Proposal #1745
Jessie's Child #1776

* The McClouds of Montana

LOIS FAYE DYER

lives on the shores of beautiful Puget Sound in Washington State. She loves to hear from readers and you can write to her c/o Paperbacks Plus, 1618 Bay Street, Port Orchard, WA 98366. Please visit her on the Web at www.LoisDyer.com and at www.specialauthors.com.

For my sisters, Norma, Shirley, Elsie and Carol,
and for my brother, B. L. Jacobson.
Because you all remember those years in Montana.

Chapter One

Wolf Creek, Montana
Early Spring

Jessie McCloud shivered in the raw wind that blew down from the buttes, carrying a spatter of raindrops that felt like ice against her tear-dampened cheeks. She struggled to stifle her sobs but succeeded only in hiccupping as she tried to swallow the sound.

Flanked by her two tall teenage brothers, she clutched their hands, squeezing harder.

Seventeen-year-old Chase bent toward her. "Are you okay, Jessie?"

She nodded, glancing fearfully over her shoulder at the Montana State Department of Corrections Officer who stood several feet behind them. The uniformed man's expression was stern, his gaze fixed on the mahogany casket and gravesite beyond.

Jessie turned back, focusing on the velvety petals of the red roses with their lush green leaves resting on top of the casket. She'd adored her Grandpa Angus and could hardly believe he was gone. No longer would he tell her stories and share the butterscotch candy he always had tucked away in his jacket pocket. No longer would he tease her and laugh at her riddles.

She looked up at her brother Luke, who held her right hand. His face was grim as he stared toward the mourners on the far side of the grave. Curious, her gaze followed his and located their grandfather's widow, Laura Kerrigan-McCloud, surrounded by her family.

Jessie's eyes narrowed over the small group of Kerrigans.

Her grandfather had married Laura Kerrigan when they were both elderly and their hair snowy-white. He'd loved her dearly and wed her despite the objections of her family and his. The feud between the McClouds and the Kerrigans had begun in 1922, when a crooked poker game cost a McCloud 2500 acres of prime land. But her Grandpa Angus was the first to die as a result of the enmity between the two families, indirect though it was.

Jessie had overheard Luke telling their father he was convinced Grandpa Angus had died of a broken heart. He loved his grandchildren and when Chase went to jail, Luke believed, Angus had grieved himself to death.

Jessie hated all the Kerrigans but the one she hated most wasn't there. Lonnie was nearly seventeen, the same age as Chase, but he was a bully, the opposite of her big brother in every way. Lonnie had caused the death of Chase's best friend, Mike Harper, in a car accident that had left Chase hospitalized with two broken ribs and a concussion. Backed by his father, Harlan, Lonnie had lied and convinced the police and courts that Chase had been the driver of the wrecked pickup truck. Chase, convicted of negligent homicide, had been sentenced to jail.

It was so unfair. She vowed to become a lawyer and send all the Kerrigans responsible for the injustice, especially Lonnie and his father, to prison. She wouldn't give up until she'd set things right.

The wind picked up, sweeping down from the buttes behind the cemetery to ruffle the short spikes of spring grass that were bright green threads among winter's dried yellow stalks. The raw breeze carried rain, and umbrellas snapped open.

"Our Father, Who art in Heaven…" The minister's voice was joined by Jessie's mother's, her tear-filled recitation of the familiar words trembling in the air. Unable to speak, Jessie gripped Luke's and Chase's hands tighter. Their much-larger hands were roughened by calluses, enfolding her cold, smaller ten-year-old fingers in warmth and security. Bracketed by her tall teenage brothers, she struggled to keep the sobs inside but the effort made her chest hurt and her eyes sting as grief clamored for release.

The prayer ended and the crowd of mourners on the far side of the casket stirred, murmuring while they lined up to follow the minister as he approached her parents.

All but the Kerrigans. Laura, Harlan and his widowed sister-in-law, Judith, and her two children, Rachel and Zach, climbed into a luxury sedan and drove off, leaving the cemetery.

I hate you all. Jessie vowed fiercely, *You'll pay for hurting my family. I swear on Grandpa's grave.*

"Jessie," her mother said softly.

A tear rolled unheeded down Jessie's cheek and she obeyed the silent invitation of her mother's outstretched arm. Releasing her brothers' hands, she moved to her mother's side and nestled against the slightly damp wool coat. Margaret McCloud slipped her arm around her daughter's shoulders and tucked her close.

The stream of mourners offering hushed words of condolence seemed to go on forever but finally the last person turned away.

"It's time, son." The corrections officer stepped forward, resting his hand on Chase's shoulder.

No! He couldn't take Chase, not now.

Jessie sucked in a breath and held it, her muscles rigid with the effort to not cry. Her vision wavered as she watched the big brother she adored hug her mother and father and say goodbye. Then it was her turn. The tears slipped past her defenses.

Sobbing, she flung herself at Chase and wrapped her arms around him, desperate to keep him with her.

Chase's tight hug and the feel of his hand as he smoothed her hair was heartbreakingly dear and familiar. She couldn't make her fingers release him but at last, he pried her fists free of his coat and stepped back.

Jessie felt ripped in two. The next few moments were a blur as her brother said goodbye. Far too quickly, the marked police car was driving away, leaving Jessie, Luke and their parents standing alone by the gravesite.

I hate the Kerrigans, she thought fiercely, fists clenched, as she stared after the police car taking her brother away.

Wolf Creek, Montana
Late summer, 15 years later

"Zach Kerrigan is back in town."

Jessie McCloud froze, all her attention focused on the voices of the women in the next grocery aisle.

"I know. Stacey saw him buying gas at Keeler's

Truck Stop two days ago. She said he hasn't changed, in fact, he looks better than he did in high school. She was almost hyperventilating while she was telling me."

Feminine laughter floated over the shelves. Jessie stood motionless in the cereal aisle, clutching a forgotten box of granola mix.

"And he wasn't wearing a wedding ring, but she didn't have a chance to ask him whether he was involved with anyone."

"I hope not," the first speaker said. "But one of us should find out. Why don't you…" The voice faded, the two women obviously moving away down the aisle.

Zach's home. Jessie felt shell-shocked. *When did he come back? How long has he been here?* She'd been out of town herself for the last two and a half weeks, visiting a college friend in Wyoming, but she'd spoken to her parents several times while she was gone. Her mother hadn't said a word about Zach's return to Wolf Creek.

"Mommy? Can we buy this cereal?"

The little-boy treble, followed by a tug on her khaki shorts, broke the spell that held Jessie and she looked down. Her three-year-old son, Rowdy, clutched a box of cereal against his middle with one arm while his right hand gripped the hem of her shorts. She forced a smile. "Sorry, Rowdy. What did you ask me?"

"Can we get this one?" He released her to grasp the box with two hands and hold it up for her inspection. The bright colors of a superhero's costumed body splashed across the front panel.

"Sorry, kiddo." Jessie shook her head. "That's about ninety-five percent sugar and five percent wheat. Let's try this one."

Rowdy scowled, clearly disappointed. "But Mom, this is what all the superheroes eat."

"And just how do you know, young man? Have you been watching cartoons with Uncle Chase and Uncle Luke again?"

"Yup." The little boy grinned, his face lighting with mischief.

He looked so much like his father in that moment that Jessie's heart clenched. The twinkle in his dark gold eyes, so unlike the color of her own blue ones, was infectious. Her smile wobbled as she ruffled Rowdy's mop of hair, her fingers lingering on the silky strands of ebony hazed with subtle highlights that echoed her own auburn mane. "I'm going to have a talk with your uncles," she warned. "They know you're not supposed to watch television."

"We only watch the good stuff," Rowdy assured her.

"Hmm," Jessie murmured. Her brothers were convinced she was too strict with her son and had taken it upon themselves to expose him to the "good stuff" they thought all little boys should know, including cartoons, with a special emphasis on Spider-Man, the Road Runner and Sponge-Bob SquarePants.

"Can we go to Uncle Luke and Aunt Rachel's house tonight?"

"Not tonight," Jessie murmured. Her brother Luke had recently married Zach Kerrigan's sister, Rachel, and Rowdy had immediately extended his adoration of Luke to include his new aunt. After the initial shock of learning her brother had fallen in love with Lonnie Kerrigan's cousin, Jessie had reluctantly been won over when Chase gave the couple his blessing. She still had reservations about whether Luke had betrayed Chase by marrying a Kerrigan, but was growing to like Rachel more each day. "Maybe tomorrow."

"Okay." Rowdy bounced down the aisle ahead of the grocery cart, jumping from one tile square to the next like a miniature human pogo stick.

Behind him, Jessie dropped the granola into the nearly full grocery cart, her mind whirling as she followed her son. Maybe Zach was only in town to visit his mother and would soon be gone. If so, their paths might not cross. Wolf Creek was a small town but perhaps if she was careful, she could avoid running into him.

But what if he were home to stay?

The possibility seemed unlikely. The Zach she'd known for one brief night four years ago had thrived on dangerous military assignments in foreign countries. It was difficult to imagine he could change so dramatically that he'd willingly settle for a quieter life in Wolf Creek. She'd been convinced he wouldn't return but now that he had, she was faced with a huge dilemma. When she'd learned she was pregnant with Rowdy four years earlier, she'd had good reasons for not telling Zach. Those reasons still existed. She could have left Wolf Creek and reduced the likelihood of seeing Zach again but she'd taken a calculated risk and returned home to build a life after law school.

It appeared her luck may have just run out.

Maybe it wasn't too late to reconsider John Sanchez's offer to join his law firm in Kalispell.

The mountain town was separated from Wolf Creek by nearly the full width of Montana. Surely she and Rowdy would be safe there?

But she hated the idea of leaving her family and her home. Besides, wouldn't her running away be one more victory for the Kerrigans?

No, she resolved in the checkout line. She wouldn't panic. Before she made any decisions, she had to find out how long Zach planned to stay. It couldn't be too hard for her and Rowdy to simply maintain a low profile and avoid him.

Once Rowdy was tucked into bed that evening, Jessie thumbed the mute button on the television control, leaving the screen lit with a travelogue, and dialed Luke's phone number.

Her brother's wife answered on the second ring.

The two chatted for several minutes about Luke, Rowdy and a legal case Jessie was working on before she found an opening.

"I heard a rumor in town today that your brother, Zach, has come home," Jessie said casually.

"Yes." Rachel's voice brightened, affection pouring over the line. "He was at the house when I returned from Denver. Didn't I tell you? I guess that by the time Luke and I got home from our honeymoon, having Zach back was old news." Her voice sobered. "I'm so glad he's here, Jessie. I wouldn't have felt comfortable leaving Mom alone to deal with Harlan and Lonnie while we were in Hawaii if he hadn't been."

"It sounds as if the timing of his return couldn't have been better. He's been back in Wolf Creek how long—a few weeks?"

"Yes, almost three and a half, actually. There's so much work to do at the ranch that he's been staying close to home. Do you know Zach, Jessie?" Rachel asked. "He probably finished high school and left town before you were a freshman."

"I think he graduated several years before I did," she said, avoiding answering Rachel's question. Jessie doubted there was a female in her age bracket who didn't know who Zach Kerrigan was.

"You'll have to come over for dinner one night this week and meet him," Rachel said with enthusiasm. "I'll see if I can drag Zach away from work for a few hours. What day would be best for you and Rowdy?"

"I'm not sure." *Never,* she thought. "I left my day planner at the office but I'll check the calendar tomorrow and let you know. I think I have a couple of evening meetings but I don't remember which nights."

"Let me know and I'll give Zach a call."

"I'll do that." She paused. "Do I need to find time this week or would next week work as well? Will he be leaving soon?" Jessie asked, holding her breath.

"I'm not sure," Rachel replied. "He told me he's staying but his boss insisted he just take a three-month leave of absence. If I have my way, Zach's home for good. I can't imagine how Mom will run the ranch without him. So, about dinner," Rachel continued, "you'll call and let me know when you can join us?"

"Yes, as soon as I check my calendar. I have a court hearing in the morning but I should be back in the office after lunch."

"Great. Talk to you then."

Jessie said goodbye and dropped the phone

into its cradle, staring unseeingly at the flickering television screen. Dinner with Zach and Rowdy at the same table?

Not a chance.

And he's here for at least three months, maybe longer, she thought. A dull headache throbbed insistently and she rubbed her temples while her mind whirled with memories.

She'd last seen Zach in Missoula, miles away from Wolf Creek on the opposite side of the state. She'd been enrolled in the University of Montana's law school; he was working in the campus Marine Recruitment Office while recovering from injuries received during an overseas assignment. Though she'd passed him on campus, they hadn't exchanged even polite hellos until late one afternoon when they both happened to be at an off-campus coffee shop. They were waiting in line for lattes when what turned out to be a disgruntled ex-employee entered, drew a gun and began to shoot. The situation was chaotic and frightening, and afterward, Jessie was shaken, terrorized by the violence. Zach had bought her dinner, then walked her across campus to her apartment, where they'd come together in a primal, life-affirming reaction to the stress and danger. Jessie had lost track of the number of times they made love but sometime during the night, she realized that the foundation of her world had shifted.

The next morning she'd been appalled at herself for sleeping with Chase's enemy. She'd said hurtful things that she knew she'd never forget, and in anger, both agreed the night had been a mistake. Zach left for the airport, bound for Afghanistan to rejoin his military unit.

That cataclysmic night had consequences neither of them had anticipated when a home pregnancy test turned out to be positive a short month later. At first, Jessie couldn't decide whether she should locate Zach and tell him their night together had had unexpected results.

The question had haunted her.

She'd spent the years since Chase went to jail vowing vengeance on the Kerrigans. Chase hadn't come home immediately after he was released. Instead, he'd taken a job as a bounty hunter with an agency owned by the brother of a prison guard he'd befriended. Up until a year ago, Chase had lived in Seattle and during his infrequent visits home, he wasn't the brother she remembered from her childhood. He seemed a hard and dangerous man employed in a violent business, his emotions locked behind an impenetrable wall. And it broke her heart. She was tortured by the guilt of betraying Chase by sleeping with the enemy. She couldn't bring herself to tell her beloved brother that his nephew's father was a Kerrigan.

But buried deep within her was the conviction that the night she'd spent with Zach had been more than an impetuous fling. Zach clearly hadn't felt the same earthshaking connection she had. Was it likely he'd have even wanted to know she was pregnant?

She couldn't imagine how she could have told her parents they'd have to share their first long-awaited grandchild with the family they hated. And how would they have felt about her baby, knowing despised Kerrigan blood ran through his veins? Jessie was convinced her parents and brothers would never purposely treat her child differently because of Zach's family, but how could she be sure the feud between the families wouldn't subconsciously color their view of her baby?

It took two long, sleepless weeks to reach a decision. In the end, she'd decided not to try to contact Zach but instead, she told her parents she'd married a fellow student in a quick Las Vegas wedding, only to divorce just as easily six weeks later. She confided the truth about the fictitious marriage only to her mother and even then, she didn't reveal the identity of her baby's father.

It had been a complicated plan but Jessie had thought it was necessary. And she'd told herself she would make the decision to tell Zach he was a father if the opportunity arose and if she thought he'd care, although she knew that wasn't likely to ever happen. Zach had left Wolf Creek at eighteen and, as far as she was aware, he'd never been back.

After she'd finished law school and Rowdy was two years old, she'd returned to Wolf Creek to set up her law practice and build a life for herself and her son.

I may have to tell Zach about Rowdy at some point, she thought, *but if I do, it's not going to happen at dinner with his sister and my brother present.*

Rachel and Luke's marriage had created a bridge between the two families, over which various members of the McClouds and Kerrigans had cautiously crossed. Jessie genuinely liked Rachel but she couldn't imagine her sister-in-law being pleased to learn that Jessie had kept it a secret that Rowdy was her nephew. Let alone how Zach would feel about the news.

The McClouds' acceptance of Rachel didn't extend to the rest of the Kerrigan clan. Jessie didn't want to contemplate how her brothers might react if they learned Zach Kerrigan was Rowdy's father. She'd refused to reveal anything about her son's biological father beyond the tale of the nonexistent six-week marriage. After that conversation, Chase and Luke had made occasional caustic remarks about "the SOB who bailed when he found out Jessie was pregnant." They'd been very careful not to make such comments in front of Rowdy, but they'd also refused to listen when she'd tried to persuade them that their interpretation was wrong.

She shuddered. Having her brothers learn a Kerrigan was "the SOB who bailed" would only make their reaction worse.

She wondered how much more difficult it would be to tell Zach.

If I decide to tell him, I'll make an appointment to see him and do it in person. She didn't relish the thought. Though she was convinced she'd moved on and put her feelings about that night behind her, she knew delivering the news about Rowdy wouldn't be easy.

Would he be angry? She hadn't a clue.

Probably not, she thought. *Statistics prove a high percentage of men in America don't have any interest in children beyond the act of conception.*

Would he want to be involved in Rowdy's life or would he choose to remain anonymous?

Ah, now that was the most important question, she realized. And the one that worried her most.

She could bear Zach's anger and her parents' disappointment in her; also, her brothers' certain outrage and Rachel's dismay. She'd been forced to make choices four years ago that impacted all of them and would pay the price for her decisions without flinching. But Rowdy was innocent. He didn't deserve to be involved in an emotional firestorm.

A swift rush of motherly protectiveness swamped her.

He's my little boy, only mine. Jessie realized

her hands were curled into fists, her entire body tensed as if ready for battle. She forced her fingers to straighten and took several deep breaths in an effort to relax.

Despite her fierce emotions, she knew her instinctive response was impractical. She was a lawyer, a member of the Montana Bar Association, and she was fully aware Zach had a right to visitation with Rowdy, if that's what he wanted. Excluding Zach from their son's life wasn't legally possible.

That didn't mean she had to like it.

She thrust her fingers through her hair, tugging the thick, heavy mass away from her temples where the dull headache still throbbed.

Worrying at this point was fruitless, she told herself. More likely than not, Zach would be gone before long, flying back to whatever part of the world was currently at war and needed his services as a munitions consultant.

She switched off the television and turned off the lights as she left the living room to walk down the hallway to her bedroom. A lamp glowed softly on the bedside table, casting shadows into the corners of the comfortable room. Jessie loved her little house and had spent hours sanding woodwork, painting walls and making it uniquely hers. The rest of the house reflected the reality that a three-year-old boy lived here but this room was her sanctuary. Here, she'd indulged herself with pale green silk curtains that matched the spread and pillow shams on the walnut four-poster bed. The bed had been her great-grandmother's and, like the matching nightstands, bureau and oval mirror, its polished surface gleamed with years of loving care.

The quiet surroundings had always had the power to soothe and relax her but tonight the room didn't calm her worries about Rowdy and Zach. Even after she'd showered, dressed in a cotton tank top and loose pajama bottoms, climbed into bed and switched off the lamp, her mind continued to whirl with all the possible ramifications of Zach's return to Wolf Creek.

When she finally fell asleep, she dreamed of Zach and the first time he'd come to her rescue. It was during the summer she was ten and he was already a tall, lanky teenager of fifteen....

The first summer after her grandfather died seemed longer and hotter than usual. Jessie and her best friend, Sarah, tried to keep cool by swimming in the stock pond and spending Saturday afternoons in the air-conditioned theater.

Following a movie one Saturday, Jessie and Sarah stopped at Muller's Candy Shoppe before meeting Sarah's mother at the library. They were contemplating a purchase when the string of bells hanging on the door jingled loudly and two teenage boys entered the nearly empty store.

"Well, well, if it isn't a McCloud. Heard from your convict brother lately?"

Jessie stiffened at the jeering tone in Lonnie Kerrigan's voice. Determined to ignore him, she resolutely stared at the glass case and the rainbow display of saltwater toffee inside. She wished Mr. Muller hadn't stepped into the back room. The bell she could use to call him back was located at the far end of the counter by the cash register, too far away for her to reach.

"What's the matter, kid? Cat got your tongue?"

He brushed past her, bumping her in the process.

"Don't pay any attention to him, Jessie," Sarah urged.

Jessie glanced sideways and saw that her

friend's eyes were fearful as she watched the blocky teenager on Jessie's other side.

"Yeah, kid. Don't pay any attention to me." Lonnie leaned against the candy display, grinning with malicious enjoyment at Sarah's concern.

"I won't," Jessie said, filled with hate and loathing for the bully. "You're not worth it."

"Is that right?" She heard the sneer in his voice. "All you McClouds are the same. You're a little young, but I'm sure it won't be long before your brother Luke joins Chase in jail." He waved expansively at the interior of the candy shop. "I'm surprised you're allowed in here without supervision. Wonder if Mr. Muller knows he's got a future criminal in his store?"

Goaded beyond endurance, Jessie turned to face him, furious. "You're a pig, Lonnie Kerrigan. You should be in jail, not Chase. You're the criminal—you and your whole family!"

She glared up at him, daring him to do anything about her harsh words. At ten, she was several feet shorter than the seventeen-year-old and he outweighed her by more than a hundred pounds. She didn't care. Three months earlier, she'd watched as Chase was handcuffed and driven away from their grandfather's funeral in a police car. She blamed Lonnie for her brother's absence and she hated him with a depth and passion she'd never before felt in her short life.

A blond teenage girl standing near the door giggled at Jessie's words and Lonnie flushed, his eyes narrowing. He stepped closer, bending toward Jessie.

"You little bitch."

Her mother would have washed his mouth out with soap for using that word. Jessie stuck out her chin and refused to back down.

He grabbed her arm and twisted. The pain was excruciating but Jessie wouldn't give him the satisfaction of seeing her cry. Instead, she glared harder, blinking back tears.

"Let her go."

Lonnie's gaze left hers and he looked over her head at someone behind her. His mouth tightened before he sneered again. "Stay out of it, Zach. This is none of your business."

"I'm making it my business. She's just a kid. Let her go."

"You taking her place?"

"If I have to."

Lonnie laughed and his grip loosened. He pushed Jessie and she stumbled sideways against the glass display case.

"Hey, none of that in here! You two take it outside if you have to fight," Mr. Muller said firmly.

Jessie glanced over her shoulder. The gray-haired, heavyset owner of the store left the doorway to the back room and leaned over the counter, frowning at Lonnie and Zach.

"Yeah, yeah," Lonnie snarled. "We're goin'."

Zach spun on his heel and stalked out of the shop, followed by Lonnie, his friend and the two teenage girls.

"Come on." Jessie grabbed Sarah by the hand and pulled her across the room and out the door in time to see the teenagers disappear into the alley. She and Sarah ran to the corner of the building and stopped, peering around the edge.

Lonnie was taller, heavier and had a longer reach than his younger cousin, who at fifteen was still rangy with lighter muscle on his fast-growing body. Within minutes, blood was oozing from Zach's nose and welling from a cut on his lip, his right eye was red and bruised. He didn't stop, however, and no matter how many times

Lonnie knocked him down, he got up and kept swinging. By the time a police officer, probably called by Mr. Muller, arrived to break up the fight, both boys were bleeding from their faces and knuckles. Their white T-shirts were ripped, smeared with dirt and stained with blood spatters.

"Wow, Jessie," Sarah said in awe as the policeman marched the battered combatants down the street toward the police station. "He stood up for you and made Lonnie leave you alone. Why did he do that?"

"I don't know. He's a Kerrigan. He probably just likes to get into fights and beat up people." Jessie was pleased that her voice sounded unconcerned and dismissive. But she was secretly amazed that Zach Kerrigan had kept Lonnie from hurting her. Why? Could he possibly dislike Lonnie and his bullying as much as she did?

Jessie woke, struggling through clinging shreds of sleep and dreams. She sat up, rubbing her hands over her face in an effort to clear away the images of her ten-year-old self watching Zach fight Lonnie in the dust of the alley behind Muller's Candy Shoppe.

The residue of half-remembered conflicted emotions churned, accompanied by the memory of Zach's battered face on that long-ago afternoon.

Had he saved her that day because he was being kind to a child being bullied? Or had he simply taken advantage of an excuse to fight Lonnie? It was no secret that the Kerrigans often exploded into physical violence.

She tipped the bedside clock so she could read the time.

"Two o'clock? Ugh." She lay down, punching her pillow. She had to be at the office by seven and made a mental note to brew extra-strong coffee in the morning.

Chapter Two

Zach Kerrigan slid out of the booth in the back of the coffee shop and stood, settling his straw cowboy hat on his head as he walked to the front of the restaurant. He'd been absent from Wolf Creek for years but several ranchers seated at the booths and tables nodded hello as he passed. He returned the silent greeting, recognizing a few of the older men.

He stopped at the front counter, waiting for the waitress who'd served him to hurry forward. She stepped behind the cash register and he handed her his check and several bills.

"Keep the change."

"Thanks." She flashed him a quick, appreciative smile. "You're new in town, aren't you?"

"Not exactly," he drawled. "I grew up here."

"Really?" She cocked her head, eyeing him curiously. "Why haven't I seen you in the restaurant before?"

"I've been away." Zach slipped his wallet into his jeans' back pocket, glancing sideways as the door opened.

The woman who stepped over the threshold was young, her slim shape clothed in a conservative cream business suit. Her face was turned away from him as she spoke to the man behind her, giving Zach a view of deep auburn hair and the pure lines of her profile.

His memories of Jessie McCloud were vivid and powerful but the woman in front of him was even more beautiful than he'd remembered. A slam of pure longing, lust and need rocked him. He'd expected the lust. The instant ache of yearning need stunned him.

She laughed at a low-voiced comment from

the older man and turned, taking two steps into the café before her gaze met Zach's and she abruptly halted.

Her eyes widened and her face paled. Emotions moved swiftly across her expressive features— shock and stunned surprise, quickly followed by a brief glimpse of what Zach thought was raw pain. Then her eyes shuttered and her face smoothed, concealing what she'd just revealed as effectively as if she'd drawn a curtain closed.

"Zach." The faint inclination of her head was polite, her voice cool and distant.

"Jessie." He touched the brim of his hat, his gaze flicking to the elderly man standing at her elbow. He didn't recognize him, but the Stetson, jeans and boots he wore marked him as a rancher.

The man nodded politely. In the moment it took for Zach to nod in response and return his attention to Jessie, she'd walked away from him toward the back of the café.

Ignoring the curious glance from the man with her, Zach left the café. He strode down the sidewalk toward the feed store, oblivious to the people he passed and the sound of traffic on the street.

He'd thought about Jessie more often than he

cared to admit during the last four years, and in the weeks since he'd returned to Wolf Creek, she'd haunted his dreams every night.

He hadn't expected her to welcome him with open arms, but neither had he thought she'd turn and walk away as if she hated the sight of him.

"Zach!"

He looked up and cursed silently. Harlan Kerrigan stepped out of his office and stood only yards in front of him. Zach, not yet ready to deal with his uncle, had ignored the messages Harlan had left on his answering machine. He still didn't want to talk to the man.

But he closed the distance between them. "Afternoon, Harlan."

"Afternoon, Zach. I've been wanting to talk to you."

"Sorry, I've got a sick horse I have to check on. Maybe some other time."

Harlan's mouth tightened, his ruddy complexion darkening. His eyes reflected his annoyance but he surprised Zach when he didn't insist. "Let's make it soon."

Zach nodded and went his way.

What the hell is Harlan up to? It wasn't like him

to give up easily. Zach made a mental note to ask his mother and sister if Harlan had approached either of them and if he had, what he'd wanted from them.

Seated in a booth in the café, Jessie reined in her emotions, slammed them into a locked corner of her mind and focused on lunch. Ed Sanders was an old friend of her father's and when he'd called her office for an appointment to update his will, she'd been delighted. They finished his legal work just before noon and his offer to buy her lunch was a welcome diversion. She hadn't given a thought to the possibility of running into Zach.

So she'd been totally unprepared when she did. The shock and heartache that followed had nearly paralyzed her. The only response she could manage was a brief greeting followed by a swift escape to the back of the café.

She managed to chat and laugh at Ed's jokes but when she returned to her office after lunch, she had no clear memory of their conversation.

"Hi, Jessie." Tina, the single mother of three who expertly ran the business side of Jessie's law office, looked up and smiled when Jessie entered. "How was lunch?"

"Fine." Jessie murmured her thanks when Tina handed her several pink phone message slips. She glanced quickly through them. "The Auditor's Office didn't call back with the information on Dad's title search?"

"Not yet. Would you like me to check with them again?"

"That would be great, thanks, Tina." Jessie was legal counsel for McCloud Enterprises and the work often involved property acquisitions. The latest negotiation for a thousand acres of ranch-land was proving tricky due to a potential clouded title issue. Her father was impatient to finalize the deal and she wanted the situation resolved as quickly as possible.

Tina picked up the phone and dialed as Jessie crossed the reception area and walked into her office, closing the door behind her. She dropped the message slips on her desk and sat in the comfortable leather chair, pulling open a bottom desk drawer to slip her purse inside.

Alone, behind the closed door, at last she allowed herself to think about her encounter with Zach.

He seemed the same, yet somehow different. The moment she'd turned and looked into his eyes, she'd been blindsided by the emotions that roared through her.

Why am I not over him? She closed her eyes, but the vivid image of Zach standing in the sunlit café was seared on the inside of her lids.

He'd worn a straw cowboy hat tugged low over his brow, his black hair long enough in back to curl against the collar of a blue chambray work shirt. Clean faded Levi's hugged the length of his long legs, a worn black leather belt threaded through the belt loops and black cowboy boots covered his feet.

His eyes were dark gold, carbon copies of Rowdy's. But while Rowdy's were filled with innocence and mischief, Zach's were unreadable beneath the arch of dark brows. He was deeply tanned, his skin a darker brown than her father's and brothers', who spent long hours outdoors and Jessie wondered if he'd been called home from some far-off desert country.

She'd almost forgotten how big he was, or maybe she'd blocked the memory from her mind. She'd felt tiny looking up at him, even in the high-heeled shoes she wore. He was over six feet tall, with broad shoulders and chest, powerful arms and a narrow waist.

And he still had that seductive scent that could only be described as male. Whatever the elusive scent was, she'd felt its impact in the café, even though she'd stood four feet away from him.

Dear God. She raised trembling fingers to her lips. *I can't have feelings for him. I can't.*

The intercom buzzed and she drew a deep breath, willing her voice not to quaver. "Yes, Tina?"

"I've just received the trust fund data for the Michaelson Estate. Would you like me to bring you the file?"

"Yes, please." Jessie quickly smoothed her fingertips over her lashes and down her cheeks to erase any evidence of tears, and picked up a pen.

By three that afternoon she closed the file atop her desk in frustration, unable to concentrate. Pleading a headache, she asked Tina to cancel her four-thirty appointment, left the office and went home to change out of her suit and heels and into cool green shorts. She pulled a white tank top over her head, slipped her feet into leather sandals, and collected Rowdy from next-door neighbor

Mabel Harris's loving care before escaping town to drive to her parents' ranch.

The one place on earth she could be assured she wouldn't see Zach Kerrigan was on McCloud land. A less self-assured person might call the visit to her parents blatant hiding. Jessie preferred to call it strategic maneuvering.

Chapter Three

Wolf Creek was a small town. Fifteen minutes after backing out of her garage, Jessie was driving north through open ranchland, the paved two-lane road she traveled lined on each side with barbed wire fences. On the far side of the fences lay mile after mile of open pasture and flat-topped buttes. The land was dotted with grey-green sagebrush while swathes of verdant brush and trees followed the winding path of an occasional creek. Cattle and horses grazed or plodded along narrow tracks, marking the landscape with their brown, white and black coats.

The afternoon sun poured through the SUV's windows and Jessie switched off the air-conditioning, opting to roll down the windows of her four-wheel-drive Chevy Tahoe and let the sage-scented wind tangle her hair.

"Whee."

She glanced in the rearview mirror. Rowdy laughed, his face crinkled with delight, eyes narrowed against the sweep of wind, his hair blowing straight back from his forehead. A rush of amusement and love rolled over her. Despite the changes he'd caused in her life, she'd never regretted for an instant that he'd been born. From the moment she'd learned she was pregnant, her son had become the focus of her world. He enriched each day with a depth of quiet joy she'd never known before.

She popped a classic rock CD, one of Rowdy's favorites, into the stereo and turned up the volume. Within seconds "Ruby Tuesday" by the Rolling Stones filled the SUV and Rowdy sang along, his voice warbling the higher notes as the big vehicle ate up the miles.

Fifteen miles from town, Jessie braked, slowing to turn onto a graveled lane and past a large mailbox set solidly atop a black metal post before she drove beneath the wrought-iron arch where scrollwork spelled out "McCloud Ranch." Then she accelerated, dust billowing up behind her tires as she drove down the half-mile driveway toward the sprawl of buildings that made up the headquarters for her father and brothers' ranching enterprises. The roadway curved between white-painted wood rail fences and horses lifted their heads to watch with curiosity as the SUV passed, their glossy hides gleaming under the hot sun.

Two big pickup trucks with the McCloud logo on the doors sat in front of the main horse barn and Jessie wondered if both her father and Chase were inside. She parked just outside the elaborate gate set into the wrought-iron fence surrounding her mother's prized garden. Within the enclosure, the grass glowed a brilliant emerald green while dozens of rosebushes spilled crimson, pink, yellow and white blooms over the black metal of the fence in an extravagant display. A giant old maple tree stood in one corner of the yard, its thick branches shading one edge of the sprawling house and its deep porch, brushing against the windows of the second-story bedrooms.

A rottweiler rose and stretched lazily, barking twice in welcome as Jessie slid out from behind the wheel.

"Hey, Muttly."

The big dog woofed again and sat, tongue lolling, his attention trained expectantly on her car.

As Jessie unhooked Rowdy from his car seat, her mother came out of the house and onto the porch, drying her hands on a dish towel.

"Jessie." Pleasure filled her voice and was echoed in her wide smile. "What a nice surprise."

"Hi, Mom." Jessie swung Rowdy out of the SUV and leaned back in to collect her bag. By the time she closed the door, Rowdy had already unlatched the gate and was racing up the walk toward Margaret, arms outstretched, chortling with glee.

Jessie followed him, pulling the gate closed behind her, and laughed when Rowdy dashed up the shallow steps to fling himself at his grandmother. Margaret caught him, swung him off his feet and hugged him tight before setting him down to be greeted by Muttly. The big dog and the little boy were equally overjoyed to see each other and Rowdy threw his arms around the dog's neck. With Muttly sitting and Rowdy standing, they were nose-to-nose and Muttly licked the little boy's face in response to his exuberant hug.

"Muttly, stop that," Jessie protested.

Margaret grinned and bent to wipe Rowdy's face with the damp towel she held. Rowdy twisted away from her, intent on petting the dog.

"Come inside and we'll wash your face, Rowdy." Margaret pulled open the screen door and Jessie followed Rowdy and Muttly into the cool interior. The four of them trooped across the tiled foyer and turned left, bypassing the spacious wood-paneled living room with its leather sofas, thick wool rugs and Remington artwork, and followed the hallway to the airy kitchen.

On the far side of the room, sunshine poured through the windows of the dining alcove that looked out on the back garden. Jessie crossed to the sink, dampened a towel and squirted liquid soap onto it. "Come here, Rowdy. Let's clean you up so Grammy can give you a cookie and a glass of milk."

"I want soda," he said hopefully, his words

muffled beneath the cloth Jessie was scrubbing over his face.

"Milk," Jessie said firmly. "Have your uncles been giving you soda?"

"Not today." Rowdy smiled angelically and clattered across the kitchen to pull out a chair at the table and clamber onto it. Muttly immediately lay down beside him.

"Men," Jessie grumbled under her breath.

"I'll second that," Margaret said wryly. She opened the refrigerator, took out a carton of milk and poured some into a plastic glass that had a red-and-blue image of Spider-Man on one side.

"What's Dad done this time?" Jessie asked as she took a plate from the cupboard and collected three oatmeal chocolate-chip cookies from the vintage Dumbo cookie jar on the counter.

"He bought another airplane."

"Another one?" Jessie set the cookies and milk on the table in front of Rowdy and returned to lean against the counter. "Why does he need another plane?"

"He didn't say he *needed* it, exactly. He told me he thought it was wise to have a backup since the Cessna is fifteen years old." Margaret rolled her eyes before returning the milk to the refrigerator and taking out a frosty pitcher of tea.

"That doesn't sound totally unreasonable," Jessie said, turning to take two tall glasses from the cupboard behind her. She knew next to nothing about airplanes but her father's favorite hobby was flying and lately he'd been interested in a smaller plane a neighbor was using to dust crops. A sudden thought occurred to her and she looked at her mother. "Uh-oh. Did he buy this plane from Jack?"

Margaret nodded.

"But Jack's plane only has room for two or three people. What's Dad going to do with it?" Jessie carried the glasses to the table and returned for a plate of cookies.

"He says he's going to use it to dust the oats and rye fields down in the basin."

"Grandpa's dusting fields?" Rowdy's eyes were round with awe. "Like you dust, Mom? How does he do that?"

"No, hon." Jessie walked behind him, ruffling his hair, and took a seat at the oblong table. "It isn't like dusting furniture. When a pilot dusts fields, he flies his plane low over the ground and releases pesticide dust to kill the bad bugs that might harm the crops growing there."

"What's a pesty-side?"

"A pesticide is sort of like medicine for the crops to keep them from getting sick."

"Oh." Rowdy drained his milk. "Where's 'lizabeth, Grammy?"

"She went to town with George to buy groceries," Margaret replied.

Apparently satisfied that the McCloud family cook, whom he adored, wasn't available, Rowdy hopped down from the table. "Can Muttly and me go outside and play now?"

"Yes—but stay inside the fence and don't leave Grammy's yard," Jessie called after him when he raced for the door.

"I won't," he called over his shoulder as he pulled open the glass door and bounded out with the rottweiler beside him.

"What I wouldn't give for some of his energy," Margaret said, smiling fondly as she watched boy and dog race off across the grass.

"Me, too." Jessie took a bite of cookie, grinning when Muttly returned a thrown stick and bowled

Rowdy over before he popped up, laughing, to cast the stick again. "He's amazing, isn't he?"

"Of course. And perfect, too," Margaret stirred her iced tea and chuckled at the sight of Rowdy and Muttly playing fetch. "He's my grandson."

"Not that you're prejudiced or anything," Jessie said wryly.

"Of course not." Margaret sipped her tea, took a bite of cookie and chewed, her eyes narrowing with consideration. "I wonder how soon Luke and Rachel will have children? Have they said anything to you?"

"Not a word. But the ink is barely dry on their wedding license, Mom."

"I know." Margaret sighed wistfully. "It's so much fun having little ones in the family, I'm hoping they'll decide to have children sooner rather than later."

"Rowdy would certainly love it if they did. He's always asking me why his friend Cody has two brothers while he doesn't have even one."

"And what do you tell him?"

Jessie shrugged. "That he has two uncles and Cody doesn't have any so if he'll share Chase and

Luke with Cody, maybe Cody will share his brothers with Rowdy."

"And he thinks that's a good solution?"

"He says Cody should share his brothers but he's reluctant to agree to sharing his uncles."

Margaret laughed out loud. "Sounds like a McCloud."

"Yes," Jessie agreed. "That it does."

"Speaking of brothers, Luke told your father that Rachel's brother, Zach, has returned to deal with the property he inherited from his grandfather. I think Rachel and Judith plan to combine their acres with his and he'll manage all of the ranches together."

Jessie flinched inwardly at the mention of Zach's name but answered with relative calm. "I know, I heard the rumor in town and Rachel confirmed it."

"Did she say if he's here permanently?"

"I don't think she knows for sure although she did say she hopes he'll stay." Jessie's gaze followed Rowdy and Muttly as they wrestled and rolled on the lawn outside. "Her mom has the house in town and now that Rachel and Luke are living in his house, Rachel seems relieved to have her brother on-site."

"That makes sense. I don't know much about Zach except that he and Luke were involved in a few fistfights during high school. And he's a Kerrigan, of course, which automatically makes me distrust him. For all I know, he could be as bad as his uncle and cousin."

"You don't think there's a chance he might be more like Rachel?"

"It's possible, I suppose." Margaret's expression turned thoughtful as she considered Jessie's words. "But not very likely, given Zach grew up living in the same house as his grandfather and his Uncle Harlan. Zach's dad died when he was quite young and he had only Harlan and his grandfather as male role models. Boys tend to grow up to be a lot like their fathers, or in Zach's case, substitute fathers."

"I know." Jessie stared at Rowdy, chasing Muttly on the lawn outside the big kitchen window. "And I can't help but wonder how that inescapable truth will impact Rowdy, growing up as he is without a father in his life."

Margaret was silent for a moment, then she

leaned across the table and covered Jessie's hand with hers. "First of all, Rowdy has wonderful role models in both your brothers and your dad. Are you considering searching for Rowdy's biological father to tell him he has a son?"

"Do you think I should contact Rowdy's father?"

"I thought he should have been informed as soon as you found out you were pregnant. I know you had your reasons for concocting a fake marriage to explain your pregnancy to the family. However, unless Rowdy's father was an ax murderer or something equally bad, I think he should be told. Not just for his sake, but also for Rowdy's." Margaret paused, her gaze searching Jessie's. "Has something changed? Are you seriously thinking of trying to find Rowdy's father?"

Jessie looked down at her mother's hand over hers. She couldn't, and wouldn't, lie to her but neither was she ready to tell her the entire, complicated truth. "Let's just say I'm wondering whether it's possible, or fair, to keep Rowdy from his father forever."

"Hmm," Margaret murmured. "Is this man someone who would want a son?"

"We never discussed children or our views on being parents," Jessie said truthfully. "So I don't have any hard evidence to believe he wouldn't want to be involved in Rowdy's life."

"So you *are* considering contacting him?"

"Yes."

"Why now?"

A frisson of alarm shivered up Jessie's spine. She didn't want her mother to guess the truth about Rowdy and Zach before she was ready to explain. "What do you mean?"

"Did Rowdy say something to make you question your decision to keep his father out of his life?"

"I didn't exactly decide to keep his father out of his life forever, Mom. Contacting him before Rowdy was born would have been possible but given his work and where he lived, it would have been beyond difficult to work out any kind of visitation," Jessie said. "But Rowdy's questions about Cody and his siblings did raise the next obvious question for me—what will I say when Rowdy asks me why he doesn't have a daddy in the house like Cody has."

Margaret nodded in sympathetic agreement.

"He's bound to ask, I suppose. He's at the age where he's becoming more aware of his surroundings, and family is a big part of his life. His own family, plus the families of his little friends, are the people he spends the most time with so it's logical that his greatest curiosity centers around siblings, daddies and mommies."

Jessie sighed. "That's exactly what I've been thinking. Yesterday he asked me why Cody's mommy lets him have hot dogs for lunch and I spent fifteen minutes trying to explain why a peanut butter and jelly sandwich is more nutritious."

Margaret laughed, her blue eyes twinkling with amusement.

The sound of boots on tile interrupted them and Jessie glanced over her shoulder as her father walked through the hall archway and into the kitchen, followed by her oldest brother. The men were both well over six feet tall, and Chase's black hair, light-blue eyes and handsome face was just a younger version of his father's.

"Hi, Jessie." John McCloud's deep voice echoed the smile that lit up his weathered face. He crossed the room and bent to drop a kiss on her forehead before pulling out a chair. "Where's Rowdy?"

"Outside, playing with Muttly," Jessie said as her dad dropped into a chair next to Margaret.

John looked out the window, a grin curving his mouth at the sight of his grandson and the big dog together on the lawn.

"Are you drinking coffee or iced tea, Dad?" Chase's voice was faintly gravelly but had the same deep timbre as his father's.

"I think I'll have cold tea." He looked at his wife and shook his head. "It's too damned hot outside for coffee."

"John, no swearing."

Jessie smiled at her mother's automatic response and her father's swift grimace.

"Sorry, hon."

"What are you doing away from your office in the middle of the afternoon on a weekday, Jess? Playing hooky?" Chase set a tall glass half-filled with ice in front of his father and an identical glass at an empty spot next to Jessie. He pulled out the chair and sat down before reaching for the pitcher of cold tea.

Jessie shrugged. "I decided it was too nice a day to spend inside a stuffy office. One of the perks of being self-employed."

"True." He deftly swiped the remaining cookie from her plate and took a bite.

"Hey. That's mine."

"Not now it isn't." He grinned at her and popped the rest of the cookie into his mouth.

Jessie frowned at him, shrugged and turned to her father. "Mom told me you have a new plane, Dad."

John's eyes lit up. "Yeah." He launched into details while Jessie listened, nodding on occasion.

"Jessie," Chase interrupted after several minutes, pointing out the window. "Did you tell Rowdy he and Muttly could dig a hole in Mom's flower bed?"

"What?" Jessie followed his gaze and jumped up. "Oh, no! That boy…!"

The three left sitting at the table watched her run out of the kitchen and dash across the lawn to where Rowdy and the big dog were industriously removing rich soil from the flower bed to make a dark pile on the green grass.

"He reminds me of you at that age, Chase," Margaret commented, laughing out loud when Rowdy looked up and grinned angelically at Jessie.

"You mean because he gets in trouble with his mother too often?" A rare smile curved Chase's mouth before his eyes narrowed consideringly over the three outside. "Is everything okay with Jessie, Mom? It's not like her to skip off work."

Margaret sighed. "She's worrying about Rowdy needing his father in his life."

"Why the hell does he need his father?" Chase shot back, frowning. "The guy bailed on Jessie when she found out she was pregnant. That's not the kind of responsible parent the kid needs."

"You and Luke keep saying he abandoned her," Margaret said. "But Jessie has told you repeatedly that she couldn't reach him to tell him about Rowdy."

"It's all the same in the end, isn't it? The bottom line is, the SOB didn't make sure Jessie didn't get pregnant. I'd like five minutes alone with him in a locked room. Ten minutes would be better."

"If I ever find him, you'll have to take a number and stand in line." John McCloud's face was set in hard lines.

"Men." Margaret heaved a long-suffering sigh.

"Why is it you all seem to think a fistfight will solve everything?"

"Not everything," her husband corrected. "But sometimes, it can go a long way toward getting justice."

"Who's getting justice?" Jessie asked.

Chase looked over his shoulder. "Justice is the one thing everyone deserves."

Jessie looked puzzled but Rowdy squirmed, tugging against her hold on his arm and distracting her. "Mommy, why do I have to wash my hands and face? I'll just get dirty again when I go back outside to play with Muttly."

"I'm sure you will. But before you get dirtier, we're going to wash off the current layer of dirt. And what do you say to Grammy for digging in her flower bed?"

"I'm sorry, Grammy," he said sweetly. "Don't be mad at Muttly, either. We were looking for the bone he buried."

"Muttly buried a bone in my flower bed?" Margaret asked, surprised. "How do you know?"

"He told me."

"He did?"

John and Chase exchanged amused grins.

"Yup." Rowdy nodded, his voice muffled as it disappeared under the damp washcloth. "Muttly talks to me a lot."

"I see."

All four adults hid smiles and listened with interest to Rowdy's recital of prior conversations with the big dog.

Jessie spent the rest of the day at her parents' house and finally drove home after seven that evening. She would have stayed longer but if Rowdy wasn't in bed by eight o'clock he'd be tired and cranky throughout the following day.

There were no messages on her answering machine and she breathed a sigh of relief.

Don't be silly, she chided herself. *Did you expect Zach to call? He probably hasn't given you a second thought since he boarded that plane nearly four years ago.*

The idea didn't console her and she wasn't sure if she was relieved Zach hadn't called, or disappointed that he hadn't immediately tried to contact her. She decided to ignore the niggle of disappointment and told herself she was glad he hadn't left a message.

* * *

Two days later, Jessie was halfway between town and her parents' ranch, on her way to pick up Rowdy after work, when her cell phone rang.

She rummaged in her bag on the passenger seat beside her, found her phone, glanced at the caller ID and smiled as she lifted it to her ear.

"Hi, Mom. What's up?"

"Jessie, I'm glad I caught you before you drove all the way out here. I wanted to let you know that Rowdy isn't here."

"He's not? Where is he?"

"Luke and Rachel were by this afternoon and took him back to their house to show him the new miniature horse Luke gave Rachel."

Apprehension filled Jessie but she chatted with her mother for a few more minutes before hanging up as she neared the turnoff for Luke's ranch. She sped down the lane to the cluster of buildings that made up the headquarters of McCloud Ranch Number 6. A strange pickup sat on the far side of Rachel's car, and Jessie's nerves stretched tighter, fluttering with foreboding.

She slipped out of the SUV and slammed the door, hurrying up the walkway to the house.

"Come in." Rachel's voice answered her swift rap on the screen door and Jessie stepped inside the entry hall, cool and dim after the glare of hot sunshine outside.

"Rachel?" she called. "Where are you?"

"We're in the kitchen, Jessie. Come on back."

The murmur of Rachel's lighter tones mixed with deeper male voices reached Jessie's ears, making her heart pound in panic as she walked swiftly down the hallway, her heels tapping on the polished wood flooring.

She reached the kitchen and stopped abruptly, eyes widening as she saw the quartet seated at the table.

Luke lounged beside Rachel, who was handing an apple slice to Rowdy, perched on the chair between his Aunt Rachel…and Zach.

A less observant person might have thought Zach, like Luke, was relaxed. He sat with one arm slung over the back of the oak chair, seemingly at ease. But Jessie knew better.

One look in his eyes told her everything. They blazed with anger, accusation and something deeper, darker, an emotion she couldn't identify.

He knows. Her gaze flicked to Luke and Rachel,

but their faces reflected no knowledge of anything amiss.

"Hi, Mommy." Rowdy clambered down from his chair to race across the room.

Jessie caught him and swung him up in her arms, eyes closing briefly as he squeezed her hard before pushing back to beam at her.

"Look, Mommy, I have another uncle."

Zach's eyes flared before narrowing over her. If Jessie were the type of woman to be intimidated by big, fierce-looking men, she would have been shaking in her three-inch heels. Fortunately for her, she'd been raised with a father and two brothers whose appearances echoed Zach's.

"I see," she said calmly.

"This is my brother, Zach," Rachel said. "And Zach, this is Luke's sister, Jessie."

"We've met." Zach's voice was a low growl.

"You have?" Rachel's lift of eyebrows reflected her surprise, her gaze moving from her brother to Jessie and just as quickly back again.

"Yes," Jessie said calmly, refusing to look away from his hard gaze. "How have you been, Zach? Still dodging bullets in foreign countries?"

Chapter Four

"Not anymore." The slight curve of his lips wasn't quite a smile and it wasn't reflected in his eyes. "I'm back."

"To stay?" She couldn't believe Zach would ever return permanently to Montana and settle into the quiet life of a rancher.

Zach shrugged. "Hard to say."

"He's staying," Rachel declared firmly. "Mom and I are determined to keep him away from war zones and here at home." She looked pointedly from her brother to Jessie, not bothering to hide her speculation at the interchange between the two.

Jessie pretended not to notice Rachel's interest and glanced at the clock on the wall above the stove. "Look at the time—it's after seven already and Rowdy's bedtime is at eight. We need to get going." She swung the little boy to the floor, purposely avoiding Rachel's curious gaze and refusing to look at her brother. "Where's your backpack, kiddo?"

"On the porch." Rowdy yawned and rubbed his eyes.

"Did you have a big day playing with Muttly?" Jessie asked, smoothing her hand over his hair.

"Yes." He leaned against her side, his eyes drowsy.

"I'm afraid he missed his nap this afternoon," Rachel admitted, standing to cross the kitchen to the back porch. "He wanted to see my new horse."

"Ah." Jessie nodded. "Mom told me Luke bought you a new pet." She felt Zach's unwavering stare but didn't look at him, choosing instead to focus on Rowdy and pretend all was normal. "We'll have an early night, then."

"Don't want to." Rowdy frowned at her, the effect spoiled by another yawn. "I want to stay here and play with Uncle Luke and Uncle Zach."

"Maybe tomorrow," Jessie soothed, glancing up when Rachel reentered the room carrying a toddler-size blue backpack and set it on the table. "Are all of his toys and his blanket inside?"

"My blanket and Elmo are in the living room," Rowdy interjected.

Zach stood and held out his hands to Rowdy. "Why don't I carry you out to the car while your Mom gets your stuff?"

The little boy didn't hesitate. Jessie's heart wrenched at the easy trust with which Rowdy lifted his arms. Zach swung him off his feet and perched him on his hip. Rowdy wrapped his arms around Zach's neck and gave his mom a sleepy smile. Zach's mouth was set in stern lines, but the two male faces, one barely past the baby stage and the other all testosterone-charged adult, were astonishingly similar. Two pairs of gold eyes, rimmed with black lashes, watched her.

Jessie glanced quickly at Rachel and Luke, relieved to see both of them were looking at her instead of Zach and Rowdy. Luke's expression was puzzled while Rachel's was intrigued. Fortunately, Jessie sensed their interest was spiked by her abruptness with Zach and not the resemblance between Rowdy and his father.

"I'll get Elmo," Luke said as Zach walked out with Rowdy in his arms.

"Don't forget his blanket," Jessie called to Luke.

He reappeared almost immediately and handed the stuffed red toy and blanket to his sister.

Outside, Jessie leaned into the SUV and turned on the engine, raised the windows and switched the air conditioner on to cool the interior while Zach snapped Rowdy into his car seat. She turned up the volume of Rowdy's favorite Sesame Street CD and shut the driver's door on Elmo's crooning.

"Good night, you two," she called, raising her voice to be heard by Luke and Rachel, who stood on the porch. They waved in response and she turned to watch Zach tousle Rowdy's hair and step back, closing the door.

"I'll follow you home." He pinned her with a hard stare across the top of the SUV. "We need to talk."

"No, we don't. We said all we needed to four years ago in Missoula. In case you've forgotten that conversation, we agreed there was no future for us and there would be no ongoing communication. No phone calls, no letters, no e-mails. Nothing."

"That was before Rowdy."

"How does that change the situation?"

"You should have told me." Anger vibrated in his voice.

"You should have asked," she shot back.

Jessie glanced through the window and found Rowdy watching her, his eyes wide with curiosity and concern. She knew he couldn't hear their voices over the sound of the music but he obviously read her expression. She forced a smile for him and looked back at Zach.

"I'm not having this conversation in front of Rowdy." She crossed her arms defensively. "I'm not saying we shouldn't talk. Just not now. He'll be tucked in bed and down for the night in an hour. If you want to come by the house, we can discuss this when I know he's asleep and won't hear us."

A muscle flexed in Zach's jaw. "You haven't told him anything about me?"

"No."

She saw the fury in his eyes and the leashed tension in his body. "I'll be at your house by nine o'clock. That should give you plenty of time to put him to bed." The words carried an implicit warning.

Jessie nodded, silently watching as he turned his back and stalked to his truck, the gravel crunching beneath his boots.

She waved goodbye to Luke and Rachel, who still stood on the porch, before she slipped behind the wheel of her vehicle and fastened her seat belt.

Zach's truck reversed and then stopped while he waited for her to precede him. Jessie drew in a deep breath, her thoughts racing as she shifted into gear and drove away from her brother's house.

She was convinced she'd made the right decision when she hadn't told Zach about Rowdy.

Zach probably won't agree. She looked in the rearview mirror. The big silver pickup remained a steady six-car lengths behind her, Zach's expression fortunately unreadable at this distance. When he turned onto a side road and disappeared from view altogether, Jessie exhaled with relief.

* * *

Zach drove away from Rachel's house seething with anger and shock. He hadn't had to ask Jessie if Rowdy was his child nor had she bothered denying the little boy was his.

Rowdy was three years old. She'd had more than enough time to tell him they shared a child.

He tightened his grip on the steering wheel. Had she thought he wouldn't care he had a son? Did she plan to refuse him contact with Rowdy?

She'd better get over that idea. I'm going to be in his life whether she likes it or not.

The fact that he had a child was difficult to grasp. He'd long since given up believing he would have a family and children one day. The life he'd lived after high school, both in the military and later as a munitions consultant, wasn't conducive to having a family. A wife and children didn't integrate well into the globe-trotting schedule and dangerous assignments he and his cohorts lived. Those who had tried usually ended up divorced; there were few exceptions.

But you're a rancher now, a small voice reminded him. *You can choose to live a quiet, normal life.*

Nevertheless, he couldn't erase his past. He knew from experience that making a living from violence changed a man. Given the choice, he may never have decided to have children but now that he knew he had a son, he'd be a good father. Hell, he'd be the best father in Wolf Creek.

He parked near the gate to his house and stepped out.

"Hey, Zach."

He looked over his shoulder. Charlie Ankrum walked toward him from the barn, his shirt and jeans stained with dried mud.

"Charlie," Zach replied, slamming the truck door. "What happened to you?"

"The pump in the east pasture wasn't shutting off like it should. The water trough spilled over and made a helluva mud hole around it." Charlie looked down at his feet and shook his head at the thick mud caked on his boots.

"Did you get it fixed?" Zach asked.

"Yeah, but it took most of the day and a lot of cussin' before I was done." Charlie's gaze sharpened. "You don't look so good, boy. Somethin' wrong?"

"No." Zach didn't elaborate, even though he'd

grown up following Charlie around the ranch, learning how to work cattle, ride broncs and mend fence. The older man knew him too well.

"That's a lie," Charlie said amiably. "You have a run-in with Lonnie?"

"No."

"Harlan, then?"

"No." Zach met Charlie's unwavering, patient gaze and gave in. "I stopped at Rachel and Luke's place this afternoon. While I was there, Jessie McCloud showed up to pick up her son."

"So?" Charlie prompted when Zach paused.

Zach wouldn't have told his mother, or his sister, or a close friend. But Charlie was like a father to him.

"I think the boy is mine."

Charlie stared at him for a long moment. "I didn't know you and the McCloud girl were acquainted," he said at last. "I don't recall you talking about her."

"She was in college in Missoula when I was assigned to the recruiting office on campus four years ago."

"Well." Charlie took off his hat, wiped his forearm across his brow and eyed Zach, his faded blue eyes shrewd and kind. "You didn't know before this?"

"No." Zach felt a savage twist of anger. "She didn't tell me."

"Not good." Charlie shook his head. "What're you going to do about it?"

"Claim my kid."

"Good." Charlie jerked his thumb toward the barns behind him. "You want me to take care of the evenin' chores?"

"No. I have time to feed the stock with you. I'm driving into town to talk to Jessie later, after I'm sure Rowdy's asleep."

"Rowdy?" Charlie's weathered face creased in a grin. "She named the boy Rowdy?"

"Yeah."

"Does he look like you or her?"

"Both of us, I think."

"Can't wait to see the little guy." Charlie clapped a gnarled hand on Zach's shoulder. "Congratulations, you're a daddy. Wasn't sure I'd ever see the day."

"Thanks." Zach's spirits lifted at the genuine delight in the old cowboy's words.

They walked together toward the barn, Zach

listening as Charlie filled him in on the details of the east pasture's pump and further necessary repair.

He finished his chores then shaved, showered, changed clothes and was ready long before it was time to drive to Wolf Creek. He paced the kitchen floor, watching the clock hands slowly pass 8:00 p.m. and start their journey toward 9:00. Unable to wait any longer, he left the house fifteen minutes early and headed to town.

Jessie spent the hour after arriving home occupied with Rowdy's bedtime ritual of bath, stories, songs and cuddles. It wasn't until she'd tiptoed into his room ten minutes after his third request for a drink of water and found him sound asleep that she allowed herself to think about Zach.

Variations of possible conversation ran through her mind as she quickly showered and slipped into a simple white cotton skirt and a periwinkle tank top, the silky, scoop-necked blouse cool in the evening heat. She brushed her hair and left it loose. Small gold hoops at her earlobes gleamed against the auburn strands as she applied light makeup.

Finished, she ran a critical gaze over her reflection in the mirror and winced. Her eyes were shadowed with worry, her face too pale. She considered applying more color to her cheeks and dismissed the thought.

"Nothing's going to make this easier," she said aloud. Adrenaline and nerves tightened her body and she willed herself to relax tense muscles while she took several deep breaths. The feeling that her baby was in danger didn't go away, but her edginess lessened. She slid her feet into backless flat sandals and left the room.

The house was quiet now that Rowdy was asleep. Jessie didn't turn on lamps as she walked through the living room. Instead she welcomed the cloak of peace the dusk threw over her house and lawn. She tucked her legs under her as she settled into the cushions of the wicker armchair at the far end of the porch.

Then she waited, mentally composing a dozen different responses to what would surely be a confrontation with Zach. Her view of the situation was simple—she would protect Rowdy at all costs. She'd gone through pregnancy without Zach's presence, given birth as a single mother and been Rowdy's only parent for the short three years of his life. If Zach wanted to be actively involved as a father, he would have to convince her he'd be a positive influence in Rowdy's life—then she'd cooperate with him.

They had created a child together but she didn't really know him, she thought. He'd spent years in the military, carrying a weapon, no doubt shooting and being shot at, and she'd noted the faintly dangerous aura about him both at the café and again this afternoon. Did that mean he'd be less able to cope calmly with the mundane details of parenting? Those details sometimes seemed to require endless patience.

How do I know he'll always make sure Rowdy's seat belt is fastened? Will he supervise him adequately? Does he know what kind of food to give a three-year-old? Zach grew up under the influence of Harlan and Lonnie—how much impact will that have on his ability to be a good father?

Beyond her initial practical concerns was an even greater worry. If Rowdy became attached to Zach, how would he handle his father's absence if Zach left Wolf Creek for an assignment in a foreign country? How could Zach possibly be an active parent while he was traveling the globe? Granted, Rachel insisted her brother would remain in Wolf Creek, but could she and Rowdy count on Zach staying?

The possibility of heartache for Rowdy seemed inevitable…and unacceptable.

Jessie knew Zach could sue her to prove paternity. Since the results of a blood test were a foregone conclusion, the court system would eventually grant Zach visitation with Rowdy. Before that happened, however, she could use legal maneuvering to delay the process of a paternity suit.

If Zach refuses to be reasonable, she thought, *I'll use every legal twist I know to gain time.*

Dusk had deepened to night when Zach parked in front of Jessie's house and started up the sidewalk.

"Hi." Jessie rose from her wicker chair tucked into the shadows at the far end of the porch. He paused, searching for her. "Come inside." She glanced at the neighboring bungalow, where the white-haired couple seated on their porch swing watched with unabashed interest. She waved at the Harrises and pulled open the screen door.

Zach climbed the steps and walked inside,

aware of Jessie with each breath he drew. The house smelled like a combination of fresh flowers, furniture polish and a subtly scented perfume drifting from the woman who walked a step ahead of him. He followed her through the dark living room into the kitchen. The room was lit by recessed ceiling lights and the soft glow of a stained-glass lamp suspended over a small dining table in the corner. He halted just inside the doorway but Jessie crossed to the counter.

"Please have a seat," she said, pouring iced tea from a carafe into two glasses.

"This isn't a social visit."

She stiffened, going still for a moment before she carefully returned the carafe to the counter, picked up the glasses and turned to face him.

"I'm well aware of that, Zach. Nevertheless, I hope we can discuss this like reasonable adults." Her slim body was strung with tension, her features resolute. The dusting of freckles over the bridge of her nose was clearly visible against pale skin but her eyes challenged him.

"We can try for reasonable." He left the doorway and went to the table.

She nodded, crossing the room to hand him a

frosty glass and murmuring her thanks when he held her chair. The urge to bend his head to brush his lips against her silky, fragrant hair was as swift as it was unwelcome. He forced himself to walk away from her, putting the width of the table between them and focusing on the reason they were here.

"Rowdy's mine, isn't he?"

"You're his biological father, yes."

He'd known the answer and had thought he was prepared to hear it, but despite the gut-deep certainty that Rowdy was his son, Jessie's quiet confirmation sent a shock wave of emotion through him. "Why didn't you tell me you were pregnant?" His voice was sandpaper-rough, deepened from being forced past the lump in his throat.

"Why didn't you ask?" she shot back. "You knew the possibility was there."

"That's why I flew back to the States to find out, two months after I left."

Jessie was visibly stunned. "I don't believe you."

Zach shrugged. "That's up to you."

"But I never heard from you," she protested.

"I never made it to Missoula. I stopped in Denver to meet my mother and Rachel and they mentioned they'd heard one of the McClouds had gotten married. When they said the newlywed was the only daughter, I figured you must not have had any surprises from that night, so we didn't have anything to talk about."

Jessie pressed her fingertips to her temple, where a tension headache was beginning to throb, and struggled to accept what his words meant. Could it be? Could her make-believe marriage have kept Zach from contacting her? "I don't know what to say."

"You could tell me why you married somebody else when you were carrying my baby," he bit out, his eyes hard.

"I…" Jessie stopped. She couldn't tell him she hadn't been married. *What a mess.* "I can't explain—it's complicated."

"It doesn't seem all that complicated to me. You were pregnant with my baby and you married another man. Did you tell him?"

"No."

"I don't know who to feel worse for—myself or the other guy." He looked around the kitchen with its feminine touches. There was no evidence of a male influence in the room. "What happened?

Did he dump you when he found out about the baby?"

Jessie stiffened at the unconcealed sarcasm in his deep voice. "My marriage has nothing to do with you and I refuse to discuss it."

"Fine," he snarled. "Then suppose you explain why you didn't tell me when you found out you were pregnant."

"I think that should be pretty clear," she said fiercely. "We'd agreed that night was a mistake and there was no reason to talk again."

"But it turned out there *was* a reason to. You should have found me," he said, obviously holding his anger in check. "My mother and sister always have my contact information."

"Oh, right, and that was so doable," she scoffed. "No one in either of our families ever spoke and you think I should have called your mother or Rachel, and said, 'hello, I'm John McCloud's daughter and I need to contact your son. Oh, and by the way, I'm pregnant.'"

"You wouldn't have had to tell them you were pregnant."

"And what would I have said when they asked me why I wanted your address?"

"Nothing. Just because they would have been curious doesn't mean you'd have had to tell them anything."

Jessie shook her head in disbelief. "And that would have worked? No, Zach," she said with conviction. "I had to bring Rowdy back to Wolf Creek. I couldn't do anything to make your family suspicious."

"My family would have been over the moon to know I had a kid. Mom's wanted grandchildren for years."

"What about Harlan and Lonnie?"

"What about them?"

"Do you really think they would have left us alone?"

"I can handle my uncle and Lonnie."

"Yes, but you weren't here!" Jessie said with frustration, unable to make him understand. "I had to do what I thought was best for Rowdy."

"And you decided it was best to marry someone else and keep him to yourself?" The possibility that she'd decided having him in Rowdy's life wouldn't be good for their child was a bitter pill.

"No. I knew you had a right to know about Rowdy, under normal circumstances. But given the conversation we had before you left my apartment the morning after we…" Her voice trailed off.

"After we spent the night screwing our brains out?" Zach said bluntly, purposely choosing words that didn't reveal his true emotions about that night.

He watched as color flooded her face at the barrage of mental images from that unforgettable night, but her gaze didn't flinch from his. "If that's how you want to describe it, yes. The next morning, you were very definite about not wanting to see me again, as I recall. Given that," she challenged, "why would I have told you?"

Zach pushed upright and stalked across the width of the kitchen before turning to confront her. "Because that night made you pregnant, and that changed everything."

"It certainly did for me." Jessie's fingers tightened on her glass. The memories of making love with him that long-ago night were so vivid they shimmered like holographs, thickening and heating the air between them. Watching him walk across the room had her body burning with unwanted desire. The flex of his long thigh muscles beneath faded jeans, the stretch of white cotton over broad shoulders, the expanse of chest that she remembered pressed against her own. She hadn't been consumed with desire in four years. She didn't want to still crave making love with Zach Kerrigan.

"I'm guessing you hoped you'd never see me again and I'd never find out about him," he bit out.

"That's not true," she protested, although she knew his assessment was uncomfortably close to reality.

"Then why did you let more than three years go by?"

"I was crazy busy, juggling school and caring for a newborn. Then after graduation, I moved home to set up my law office, and I bought this house and remodeled it. One day melted into the next."

"And you couldn't have taken a half hour to write me a letter? Hell, Jessie, it wouldn't have taken that long. All you had to say was 'we have a son. Come home.' Six words, that's all you needed."

Her gaze met his. "And would you have come home?"

"Yes."

"And then what?"

"Then we would have had this conversation—only it would have happened three years ago." *And you wouldn't have married someone else, you would have married me.*

Jessie closed her eyes briefly, pressing her fingertips against them before looking at Zach once more. "I can't undo the past, Zach, and arguing about it is fruitless. What I need to know is where do we go from here? Now that you know about Rowdy, what do you want to happen?"

His answer didn't require thought. "I want him to know I'm his father."

Jessie paled and her lashes fell, then lifted to reveal eyes dark with emotion. "Is that all?"

"What do you mean?"

"I mean, what else do you want, specifically?"

"Specifically?" Zach barely hesitated. "I want to teach him to ride a horse and throw a baseball, pound nails and mend fence, throw a rope and change the oil in his car." He shrugged. "The usual guy stuff." *All the things I wish my father had lived to teach me,* he thought.

"Then you want to be an active part of Rowdy's life," she said carefully.

Zach frowned at her, wondering what she was getting at. "Of course I do. Isn't that what I've been saying?"

"I just wanted to be clear as to your intentions. This is going to be complicated and I wanted to know exactly how you picture yourself in Rowdy's life."

"Why is it complicated?"

"My family hates yours. Yours hates mine. All the reasons we decided to ignore the night we spent together are still valid."

"My sister married your brother. Years before that, my great-aunt Laura married your grandfather. If our families can tolerate a couple of marriages, they can tolerate us having a child."

The look she gave him was skeptical. "I haven't noticed any easing of the feud since Luke and Rachel married. In fact, I think it's made your Uncle Harlan and Lonnie worse."

Zach shrugged. "Harlan and Lonnie don't need the feud as an excuse to act like asses, although they never hesitate to use it if it serves their purpose. They're not worth worrying about."

"What about your mother—and Rachel?"

"Like I said, my mother's wanted grandchildren for years. She and my sister will be too excited over having a kid in the family to care about the tension between our families."

Jessie shook her head slowly, clearly unconvinced. "I doubt they'll be as accepting as you seem to think. Your mother may have wanted grandchildren, but I can't believe she won't care that Rowdy is half McCloud."

Zach eyed her consideringly. "And what about your family? How glad are they going to be when they find out I'm Rowdy's father?"

Jessie's gaze moved from his to fasten on her glass. "They won't be happy."

"So I'm guessing it's your own family's reaction you're worried about, not mine."

Jessie sighed and tucked a strand of auburn hair behind her ear. "I'm concerned about everyone's reaction, Zach. The gossips are going to have a field day with this. I don't want Rowdy hurt." The look she gave him was fiercely protective.

"I don't want him hurt, either, Jessie. But putting off the inevitable won't solve the problem. I want Rowdy to know I'm his father, which means both our families need to be told, too."

"It's not that simple, Zach."

"It doesn't look complicated to me."

She glared at him, her chin lifting stubbornly. "I need time to decide how to tell Rowdy, and my family, about you in a way that keeps the shock to a minimum."

"How much time?"

"A few weeks, at least."

"A few weeks, at most, preferably a lot less." Zach stalked to the table and collected his hat, putting it on and tugging it down over his brow. "And I want to see Rowdy while you're thinking up a plan."

"I don't know you well enough to turn my child over to you."

"He's my child, too."

"But he doesn't know you yet and until he's comfortable with you, and I'm convinced he's safe in your care, I won't let you see him without me present."

He stiffened, a muscle flexing along his jawline. "You think I'm going to harm him?" His voice was lethal, filled with cold anger.

"I think you're a man I spent one night with and beyond that, I hardly know you," she said stiffly.

"Given that, how can you expect me to turn Rowdy over to you?"

"I'm his father," he ground out.

"You know that. And I know that." Her gaze didn't waver from his furious stare. "But if you refuse to give Rowdy, and me, time to get to know you better so we're both comfortable with you in his life, I'll deny it. You'll have to take me to court and I don't think either of us wants to spend months fighting each other in a paternity suit."

"You'd go that far to keep me away from him?" He was incredulous.

"Not to keep you from Rowdy," she corrected. "To give Rowdy, and me, time to grow accustomed to having you in his life."

He glared at her. "No wonder there's a feud between our families. You're the stubbornest woman I've ever met."

"I'm a mother," she amended, "protecting my child. I'm not asking you not to see him. You're welcome to visit but I want to be there, too."

The silence between them stretched for so long, Jessie was afraid he was going to walk out.

"All right," he said abruptly. "I'll let you make the rules. Temporarily," he added. "And only because Rowdy might feel more at ease in familiar surroundings and with his mother nearby. But I'll be seeing my attorney tomorrow. I'm not a patient man. I won't wait forever for you to decide I'm acceptable father material."

Jessie nodded, relief flooding her. "We always go to the city park on Saturday morning at nine, before it gets too hot. You could meet us there tomorrow, if you'd like."

"I'll be there." He glanced at the door to the living room before turning back to her. "I want to see him."

Startled, Jessie felt her eyes widen. "Now? But, he's asleep."

"I don't care. I want to see him."

"He'll be tired and cranky if we wake him, Zach."

"I won't wake him."

Jessie hesitated, unsure. Then she registered the tension that held him and the emotion that had roughened his voice and her heart twisted.

"Yes, of course." She stood and led the way out of the kitchen and down the hall, quietly easing open the door to Rowdy's bedroom and stepping inside.

Zach walked past her to halt next to the bed. Moonlight poured through the window, slanting across the tangled sheets and illuminating the three-year-old. He lay with arms and legs akimbo, his favorite stuffed Elmo beside him on the pillow and a row of other stuffed animals just beyond. He was sound asleep, his hair rumpled, his face innocent and vulnerable in the pale light.

Zach stood motionless for several minutes. Then he bent over Rowdy, gently brushing a forefinger across his cheek, before leaving the room.

Jessie closed Rowdy's door and followed Zach. He strode through the darkened living room and paused at the screen door to look back at her.

"You've kept him from me for three years, Jessie. Three years I'll never get back. You should have told me." His voice was thick with turmoil and deep conviction.

He turned and walked out of the house.

The screen door slapped shut and his footfalls sounded on the porch boards, followed by the throaty growl of his truck engine. When silence replaced the fading sounds as he drove away, Jessie slumped, releasing her rigidly held muscles that had quivered with the effort to keep herself together through their conversation.

The very air in the kitchen had heated and thickened with the sexual attraction that still burned between them. She'd felt buffeted and bruised by both the sparks and the emotional stress made stronger by his outrage.

I should have told him.

Too late now, she thought, *much too late.* Now she had to deal with the mess she'd created by keeping silent for so long. Not to mention the outright lie she'd told her dad and brothers. How could she have believed a fake marriage would make it easier for them to accept her being a single mother?

Granted, the pregnancy had been difficult enough to deal with. She'd had nausea all day long, and had been always exhausted even though she'd slept ten to twelve hours a day. She'd found herself crying one minute, giddy the next. She'd been barely able to keep up with her homework—deciding how to deal with telling Zach was beyond her. She'd finally compromised—she'd inform Zach of their baby if and when he reappeared in her life.

She groaned and dropped her head into her hands.

Her grandmother had a favorite saying about chickens coming home to roost. As a child, Jessie had never understood the metaphor of chickens for troubles but as an adult, it made perfect sense. She only wished her grandmother had confided a foolproof way of solving the whole chickens-roosting scenario.

She rose and carried the two glasses, still full of tea, to the sink, then headed to her bedroom. Even a soothing hot bath didn't relax her enough to sleep, however, and she lay staring at the shadowed ceiling long after midnight, considering and discarding possible solutions to her dilemma.

Zach drove away from Jessie's house, raw inside. He'd been physically wounded in combat more than once, had almost died a couple of times and been forced to spend weeks recuperating. Gunshots and knives hadn't inflicted nearly as much pain as knowing Jessie didn't trust him with his own son.

He slammed his fist against the steering wheel in frustration. Would Harlan and Lonnie's bad actions forever taint his reputation?

Maybe I shouldn't have come back here.

He'd built a life away from Wolf Creek, free of the label attached to the Kerrigan name. He'd nearly forgotten how constricting it felt to deal with that on a daily basis.

The deserted highway stretched ahead of him, his headlights creating a tunnel through the darkness. He remembered all too clearly the emotions that drove him when he was a teenager and the last night he'd spent in Wolf Creek….

Zach strolled down the carnival midway. High school graduation was officially behind him and in three more days, he'd report to Marine boot camp. He wouldn't be sorry to leave Wolf Creek, he thought, pausing to watch grade-school kids and their parents shriek as the Tilt-A-Whirl ride sped up. He'd miss his sister and mother but they could visit him wherever the military stationed him in the future. It would give them a chance to leave Montana and see more of the world.

There was nothing for him in Wolf Creek. He wouldn't be coming back.

Marcus Kerrigan was one of the richest men in the state but Zach fully expected his grandfather to leave the entire Kerrigan Conglomerate holdings to his Uncle Harlan. If Zach ever had a fortune, he'd have to earn it himself.

And I will, he vowed. It had always seemed ironic to Zach that he was the grandson who loved the ranchland his grandfather had spent his lifetime accruing. But it was his Uncle Harlan and cousin Lonnie who would one day own it all. *And probably destroy it within ten years.*

He shook off his grim thoughts and looked about him. He wasn't in a carnival mood. He'd head for home and pack, maybe spend his last days in Montana camping out under the stars.

He was nearly to the end of the midway, moving purposefully toward the exit when someone crowed with delight, drawing his attention.

"Yay, I won!" A sandy-haired young boy at the ball-toss booth grinned ear-to-ear; beside him, a little girl who looked about five years old clapped with excitement.

"You sure did, sonny." The carnival barker grinned. "Pick your prize—anything on the second row."

"But I knocked down all the milk bottles. Don't I get one of the stuffed bears on the top row?"

"You have to knock down all the milk bottles twice in a row to get one of the big prizes. But you can choose anything you like off the second row." The middle-aged, ruddy-faced man picked up a smaller stuffed bear. "How about this one?"

"You didn't tell me I had to knock down the bottles two times to win a big prize." The little boy stood his ground.

"Look, kid. Take it or leave it." The barker dropped his amiable smile; his tone became surly.

"Come on, Bobby." The little girl tugged at the boy's arm, her face pale beneath her freckles.

"No. I won the big teddy bear, fair and square."

Zach recognized the two kids. The boy was eight-year-old Bobby Sharpe; the little girl was his sister, Cindy. Their father owned a small farm south of town and was a friend of Charlie Ankrum, who worked for Zach's grandfather and had befriended Zach after his father died.

He glanced around. The ball-toss stall was located across from a fortune-teller's tent at the end of the midway and only the unlit expanse of the dark parking lot stretched beyond. Behind them, the noisy crowd and music shifted and moved under the bright neon lights but that was several yards away and this section of the carnival was nearly deserted.

Bobby and Cindy's parents were nowhere in sight. In fact, there were no other adults close enough to intervene. Except Zach.

He didn't hesitate, changing his direction to approach the booth.

"Hey, Bobby. Is there a problem here?"

They turned, looking up at him. Both childish faces held relief. "Hi, Mr. Kerrigan." Bobby pointed at the barker behind the counter. "I won but he won't give me my prize."

"Is that right?" Zach queried.

"Just a little misunderstanding," the barker said, his tone once again amiable, his smile revealing gritted white teeth. The smile didn't reach his small eyes, however. "This young man thought he won a bigger prize than he actually did, that's all."

"What did he win?" Zach looked at the barker, keeping his voice lazy despite his instant dislike of the beefy man, whose buttons strained on the Hawaiian print shirt that stretched too tightly across his midsection.

"Anything on the second row." The man waved expansively.

Zach assessed the three shelves of prizes. The first row was crowded with cheap plastic toys, the second with small stuffed animals no taller than seven inches, but the top row had two-feet tall, plush teddy bears. "And what are the rules for winning a bear off the top row?"

"The player has to knock down all the milk bottles two times in succession."

"And did you tell him that?" Zach asked, his voice still calm.

"I'm sure I did," the man responded promptly. "And even if I didn't, the rules are clearly written on the side of the booth."

"Where?" Zach asked.

"Bottom left corner."

Zach scanned the painted canvas that made up the front of the booth on each side. He finally located the notice printed in tiny, nearly illegible letters.

"I see." He eyed the barker. "Any other rules for winning that you didn't tell my friend Bobby? Maybe posted on the back of the booth somewhere?"

"No, no, that's it."

"No rule about how many times a person can win?"

"No."

Zach turned to Bobby. "How many teddy bears do you want, Bobby?"

His eyes rounded and he glanced at Cindy, who was staring at Zach in silent fascination. "One for my sister, and one for my mom, and one for me."

Zach nodded and pulled out his wallet, took out several bills, and laid them on the wooden counter. "Your sign says four balls for a dollar. I'll take eight, to start."

The barker took his money and handed him four balls, giving him an oily smile.

With the same deadly precision he'd used to earn the title of best pitcher in Montana's high school baseball league, Zach wound up and threw. The speed and power behind the ball knocked all of the milk bottles off the stand with such force that they flew across the stand, slamming against the canvas back wall.

"That's one," Zach said, casually tossing and catching the second ball in one hand.

Bobby and Cindy yelled with enthusiasm and

within moments, a small crowd gathered behind Zach. The barker was no longer smiling, in fact, he was red-faced with anger but he didn't have the courage to refuse to let Zach play.

Zach methodically threw one ball after another until the top row of prizes was empty. Bobby and Cindy's arms were filled with plush bears and several more lay atop the counter.

"Got enough, Bobby?" Zach asked, looking down at them.

"Yeah." Bobby's face glowed with pleasure. "This is great. Thanks, Mr. Kerrigan."

"No problem, kid." Zach grabbed a fistful of the barker's loud shirt and pulled him closer. "Take this as a warning, friend. Don't rip off any kids again while you're here."

The man didn't answer, his flat brown eyes furious. Zach released him, ruffled Bobby's hair and walked away.

He nearly bumped into two adolescent girls just outside the fortune-teller's tent. They stared at him, wide-eyed. Zach instantly recognized the taller of the two by her red hair and the smattering of freckles across the bridge of her nose. Jessie McCloud's slender body and fine-boned young face held the promise of beauty equal to her mother's.

He nodded abruptly but they didn't respond, although he felt their stares between his shoulder blades as he left the colorful midway behind for the darkness of the parking lot.

Zach realized he was nearly home and, slowing, turned into the lane leading to his house, the headlights briefly illuminating the big mailbox with Z. Kerrigan in bold new letters.

That night at the carnival was the last he'd spent in Wolf Creek until recently. He'd enjoyed his last few days in Montana camping out on the land he loved, Zach remembered, then reported directly to boot camp.

The incident was brief and he doubted Jessie even registered it, but he'd never forgotten her expression of distrust and wariness at the carnival. She'd worn the exact same look on her face when the police marched him and Lonnie away from the alley behind Mullers' Candy Shoppe years earlier.

And he'd seen that look again when, in the Starbucks queue in Missoula, she'd glanced over her shoulder and recognized him standing in line behind her.

I should have been smart enough to realize there was no chance Jessie McCloud would ever trust me after what she believes Lonnie and Harlan did to Chase.

He parked outside the gate to the ranch house and headed inside. He wasn't a drinking man but before he went to bed, he downed three shots of whiskey with the fervent hope it would let him sleep without dreaming of Jessie.

Chapter Five

"Mommy, look. Uncle Zach's here." Rowdy beamed with delight.

Zach leaned against the closed door of his silver truck parked outside the open gate to the playground, his long legs crossed at the ankle. His face was shaded by the brim of his hat.

"Yes, I see, Rowdy." Jessie was determined to ignore the jolt of sexual awareness that accelerated her heartbeat and tightened her nerves. She mentally braced herself to cope with his anger. He wouldn't have forgiven her overnight. He might never forgive her and she had to remember his presence in her life was only because of Rowdy.

As they approached, he unfolded his arms, pushing away from the truck to stand facing them, waiting. His lips curved in a welcoming grin when Rowdy tugged his hand from Jessie's and ran down the sidewalk.

"Hi, Uncle Zach." He skidded to a stop, tilting his head back to look up. "What are you doing here?"

"Your Mom told me you might be at the park this morning and since I was in town on business, I thought I'd stop by and say hello. What's this?" He touched a forefinger to the miniature dump truck in Rowdy's hand.

"My truck. Wanna see what it can do?"

"Sure." Zach looked up as Jessie reached them. "Good morning, Jessie."

Jessie felt branded as his gaze moved from her face to her toes, then back up to meet hers once again. He didn't bother trying to hide the male appreciation that heated his gold eyes and softened the hard line of his mouth.

"Good morning, Zach." Her tone was as carefully polite as his had been but she knew he hadn't missed her reaction. Her pulse raced and her skin felt as if his palm had stroked it in slow exploration from her throat to her toes, lingering in between on all the curves that now ached and yearned. Damn him. Why could he still do this to her?

"I'm gonna show Uncle Zach how my trucks work in the sand. He's gonna play with me, Mom."

"Is he?" Jessie smiled and slipped the strap of his small backpack from his shoulder. "Why don't I carry this while you tell Zach about your trucks."

"Okay." Rowdy unzipped the pack and pulled out a small yellow metal earthmover. "You can use this one. Come on." He grabbed Zach's hand and tugged him along with him.

Rowdy skipped to keep up with Zach's long strides as they crossed the wide strip of lawn between the sidewalk and the park's play area. The sandbox was a large golden square in the rich green grass with wooden planks edging the sides at ground level. Zach sat on his heels on the grass while Rowdy dropped down onto the sand and began to demonstrate his toys.

Jessie followed them more slowly, stopping at

a picnic table to deposit Rowdy's backpack. The wooden seat was warm against the back of her knees and thighs below the hem of her white shorts. She took her paperback book and sunglasses from the pack, pretending to read behind the concealment of the dark lenses while she watched Zach and Rowdy.

Rowdy chattered away, explaining the complexities of moving sand and loading it into his miniature dump truck. Zach's replies were often followed by hoots of laughter from Rowdy.

Except for an older gentleman who walked a Jack Russell terrier in the far corner, dawdling in the shade of a huge maple, the park was occupied only by them. Then a car slowed and parked a short distance from Zach's truck. Three young children scrambled out and ran noisily toward the play area, followed more leisurely by a white-haired woman. Jessie and Rowdy often saw Barbara and her grandchildren on Saturday mornings. The two little boys joined Rowdy and Zach at the sandbox while their sister claimed a seat on the swing set. Barbara Ingram settled into the swing beside her granddaughter, smiling and waving hello to Jessie, who returned the courtesy.

Zach spent a few moments with the three little boys before he rose, brushing sand from his Levi's, and left Rowdy building in the sand with his friends. He stepped over the bench and sat down across from Jessie at the picnic table.

"He's quite a kid," he commented. "A great kid. You should be proud of him, Jessie."

"Thanks," she said softly, blinking back tears. Somehow, his quiet words of approval were important and eased a worry deep inside that she hadn't known was there. "He reminds me a lot of you."

"He does?" Zach looked surprised.

She nodded, welcoming the truce Zach seemed to have called in the tangled web of emotions and hostility that lay between them. "He has your eyes. And your dark hair. Your smile." A rueful half-smile curved her mouth. "In fact, the only thing about him that seems to have come from me is the auburn sheen to his hair." She lifted a brow, curious. "Isn't that how you knew who he was— because he looks like you?"

"Not at first. He told Rachel about his birthday party. I asked him how old he was, and when he told me, I did the math. Then I looked at him, really looked at him, and I knew beyond a doubt."

"Yes," she said with a small smile. "Difficult to deny with those eyes. Do you think Rachel guessed?"

"I don't think so. If she did, she didn't say anything."

"I thought she might call but I haven't heard from her."

He leaned his arms on the table and watched her. "What will you tell her if she calls?"

"I haven't decided. I'm hoping I can dodge talking to her until after I tell my parents."

"When will that be?"

"Today or tomorrow. I want to get it over with." She frowned. "You do realize that once I tell my family, it's possible my dad and brothers will come looking for you."

His eyes narrowed. "And why would they do that?"

"Because they believe Rowdy's father had a re-sponsibility to me. Despite my repeatedly telling them it's my fault Rowdy's father is absent, they insist on believing it's a male obligation to know if he's made a woman pregnant. Stubborn as they are, I'm afraid they won't listen to me when I tell them, for probably the thousandth time, that the blame is all mine."

"So I not only have to convince you I'll be a good father, I have to convince the men in your family I'm not an SOB who ran out on you when you were pregnant?"

Jessie's eyes widened. "How did you know that's what they keep repeating? Is that some sort of malespeak?"

"I don't know. What do you think?" Zach grinned. The switch from resigned interest to heartbreaker charm nearly stopped her heart.

"I think men belong to a secret club and women will never understand them," she said with conviction.

He laughed. "Most men would say you've got it backward. I've never met a guy who claimed to understand women."

"Mommy!" Rowdy skidded to a stop beside them, accompanied by the towheaded boy who'd joined him in the sandbox earlier. Both of them had grass stains on their knees and sand clinging to their shorts and T-shirts. "Can Andy come home and play at our house?"

Jessie glanced at her watch. "Yes, if his grand-mother says it's okay."

"Thanks!" The two boys charged off across the grass toward Barbara, who still kept her grand-daughter company on the swing set.

"I'll take off," Zach said quietly as they saw Barbara nod and smile at the two boys. He looked at Jessie. "I think I should be with you when you tell your family."

Startled, Jessie blinked. "That's very nice, but…no. Thank you. It's far better if I tell them alone."

"You don't have to do this alone. I don't like the idea of anyone giving you a hard time over something that involved me."

"Much as I appreciate the offer, telling them with you present would probably make it worse."

His eyes narrowed at her, impatience rolling off him in waves. He sighed. "All right." He took a slip of paper from his pocket and handed it to her. "This is my cell phone number. Call me if you need anything. I'm assuming we'll tell Rowdy to-gether as soon as the adults know?"

Jessie took the paper and tucked it into her pocket. "I'd rather he knew you better before he finds out. It's going to be a shock and I think it'll be easier for him to accept if he spends time with you first."

Zach's eyes darkened but Rowdy and Andy picked that moment to rejoin them. In the ensuing confusion of gathering backpacks and toys and chatting with Andy's grandmother, there wasn't an opportunity for private conversation.

They strolled in a group toward the sidewalk, pausing next to Zach's truck.

"'Bye, Rowdy."

"'Bye, Uncle Zach." Rowdy was suddenly shy, ducking his head. "Thanks for playing with me."

"You're welcome. Maybe we can do it again sometime."

"Really?" Rowdy's face was hopeful.

"Sure."

"Next Saturday?" he asked.

"Maybe even sooner," Zach told him.

"Yeah!" A grin lit up his little face and he let Andy pull him away.

"Rowdy, wait for me at the corner," Jessie called. The two children dutifully halted, crouching to observe an anthill next to the sidewalk. "I'll bring Andy home after lunch, Barbara."

"Thanks, Jessie." Barbara walked to her car and opened the door to let her remaining two grandchildren climb inside.

For a moment, Zach and Jessie were alone.

"The timing's bad but I have to leave town this afternoon. I'm flying to Dallas for a meeting with my ex-boss at company headquarters tomorrow. I'd cancel, but I did all the preliminary work on the contract and the Kuwaiti government insists I personally introduce them to my replacement and go over all the details. I'll be back on Monday. Are you definitely talking to your family this weekend?"

Jessie bit her lip. "Probably."

"I'll check in when I get home." He looked at her intently. "Don't tell Rowdy without me. I want to be there. And call me if you need me. For anything. Don't be so damned stubborn and independent, Jessie."

She nodded, searching his eyes. "Zach…" she began.

"Mommy, hurry up!" Rowdy and Andy were hopping impatiently from one foot to the other.

"I'll call you." Zach's voice was distant, his expression unreadable.

She nodded and turned away, unsure what she'd glimpsed in his eyes and uncertain what she would have said to him. She joined the boys as his truck door slammed and the engine turned over behind them. Both little boys waved exuberantly when Zach drove past, answering their shouted goodbyes with a lift of his hand before the silver truck disappeared down the street.

Later that evening when Rachel called, she let the answering machine pick up. But like most of the nights since she'd learned of Zach's return to Wolf Creek, her sleep was filled with dreams of Zach again. This time, she was older, a first-year law student at the University of Montana.

Jessie pulled the collar of her windbreaker higher, tucked her chin into the folds and jogged across the street separating the University of Montana campus from city retail shops. Reaching the sidewalk, she slowed and walked the last few yards to Starbucks. She pulled the door open and stepped inside, sighing with pleasure as a wave of warm air and the lush aroma of espresso enveloped her.

She joined the queue of customers waiting to

order, tugging off her gloves before she slid the windbreaker zipper down. The cream-colored wool sweater and jeans she wore beneath were more than warm enough for the heated room. She waved at a woman seated at a table near the window before facing front again.

If I had more time, I'd carry my vanilla latte across the room and join her, she thought. They sat next to each other in Civil Procedure I, a required class for first-year law students at the university. With the heavy homework schedule, however, they hadn't made time to become better acquainted outside the classroom.

Jessie pushed up her sleeve and checked her wristwatch. It was only 4:30 p.m. but dusk was already gathering outside the brightly lit coffee shop; November evenings arrived early in Missoula.

The line moved fractionally forward and Jessie shivered as a rush of cold air from the opening door followed someone into the coffee shop. The customer joined the queue behind her and the masculine scent of aftershave mingled with the aroma of coffee in the fragrant shop.

She glanced over her shoulder at the man behind her and froze. Tall, broad-shouldered, his dark hair clipped in a short military cut, his jacket unbuttoned over casual sweater and jeans, Zach Kerrigan returned her gaze without expression.

Jessie knew Zach Kerrigan was stationed at the recruiting office. She'd even seen him occasionally around campus, usually wearing a Marine uniform. They hadn't spoken; in fact, she pretended not to recognize him, but girlfriends had told her he was stationed in Missoula for light duty after being wounded overseas.

"Hi." He nodded politely, his eyes remote and watchful.

"Hi." She managed to reply before abruptly facing forward once more. Her stomach wound itself into knots. The coffee shop was crowded and standing in line with him directly behind her brought him too close. She was painfully aware of his scent, of his bulk and unless she left the lineup, she couldn't escape him. She briefly considered doing just that but her need for coffee and a stubborn refusal to cut and run kept her anchored in place.

The line continued to move slowly and the five customers ahead of Jessie disappeared until at last, she stood at the counter. Before she could give her order, however, the young man facing her paled, his expression one of horror as he looked past her. Jessie's gaze followed his and saw the door closing as the man who had just entered raised a rifle to his shoulder.

The loud report from the first shot shocked the crowded shop into silence. Then screams filled the room.

Jessie felt mired in molasses, unable to move, watching in disbelief as the man fired again.

"Get down!" Zach grabbed her. He wrapped his arms around her and they crashed to the floor, rolling until they slammed into a wall.

He lay on top of her, his weight pinning her to the floor, his body shielding hers. Her face was buried against the warm, strong column of his throat, her nostrils filled with his scent. Jessie was terrified. People dived behind upended tables and chairs for shelter. Screams ricocheted off the walls and a plate-glass window fractured, glass spraying the nearby area as it was shattered by a bullet.

Zach lifted his head fractionally and looked down at her. "Were you hit?" His breath ghosted over her lips.

"No," she whispered back.

"Good. Don't move."

He reached over her head and removed a glass and metal coffee press from the shelf, balancing it for a moment as if testing its weight. Then he bent his head, his lips against her ear. "This display case is between us and the shooter. You'll be safe if you stay here. Don't even twitch or you might draw fire."

"What are you going to do?" she whispered against his cheek.

He turned his head. He was so close she could see the gold flecks in his light-brown eyes and draw in the scent of peppermint when he answered and his breath brushed her face.

"I'm going to stand up and throw this coffee press at him."

Her eyes widened. "What if you miss?"

"I never miss." He grinned, a cocky, full-of-himself smile that reassured her more than his words did. "But just in case I do and he shoots me dead…" He covered her mouth with his.

Jessie didn't have time to close her eyes and Zach only half lowered his lids. For one brief, hot moment, his mouth took hers. And then he was gone.

She lay flat on the floor, staring upward at him as he rose to his feet with an easy fluid motion. His arm drew back, the movement a blur of speed, and the heavy coffee press left his hand. He disappeared around the end of the display case, moving fast, and the rifle cracked one more time, blasting a hole in the ceiling and showering the area with white dust.

Jessie scrambled to her knees, listening before she peered around the case. The shooter was lying facedown on the tiled floor, his hands behind him, while Zach knelt with one knee on his back, knotting a heavy cord around his wrists.

It was nearly two hours later before the police allowed them to leave the crime scene.

"I never did get my coffee," Jessie commented as they walked side by side to the corner, stopping for the red light.

"Neither did I." Zach looked down at her. "And my stomach is telling me it's way past dinnertime." He pointed down the street. "There's a nice little Italian restaurant halfway down the next block. I can vouch for the food and the coffee."

"Are you asking me to have dinner with you?"

"Sounds like it, doesn't it?" He searched her

face, then gently tucked her hair behind her ear, his fingers warm against her face in the chilly night. "Getting shot at isn't easy and the first time it happens is the worst."

"You sound as if you're speaking from personal experience."

"I am."

"Does eating make the shakes go away? The shaking on the inside, I mean," she asked.

"Sometimes. Mostly, staying busy and keeping your mind off of what happened helps."

She nodded with decision. "Then let's have dinner. I'm hungry, too."

The Italian restaurant was cozy and comfortable, the food fabulous. Jessie and Zach lingered over coffee. She told him anecdotes about law school classes and he entertained her with tales of his travels around the world with the military. Both of them purposely avoided any reference to Wolf Creek and their families. It was nearly midnight when Zach walked her across campus and they stood outside her apartment door. She slipped the key into the lock and twisted, freeing the dead bolt before she tucked the key chain into her windbreaker pocket and turned back to Zach.

"Well…" Her voice trailed off.

His gaze left hers, moved slowly over her face, dropping to her mouth, then lifting to meet her eyes once more. "I probably won't see you again. I'm leaving tomorrow."

The swift stab of regret at his words took her by surprise. "You're leaving? Where are you going?"

"Back to my unit in Afghanistan. The only reason I've been stationed in Montana is because I was wounded and sent here for light duty while recovering."

"Oh. But tomorrow…" She shrugged helplessly. To have gotten to know him so briefly and then for him to leave so abruptly was somehow disturbing. "Is there some sort of shooting-stress-related thing that connects a person to a fellow victim?"

He grinned, a lopsided, sensual curving of his lips. "Could be. Or it could be—" he stepped closer, slipped his arms around her waist and lowered his head "—this," he murmured against her lips.

Then he kissed her and all the heat she'd felt in that brief meeting of their mouths for that split second in Starbucks returned a thousandfold. The longer he kissed her, the more she yearned. The more she wanted. She slid her fingers into his hair and held him closer, opening her mouth beneath the urging of his.

He eased her back against the door and she welcomed the fierce press of the hard angles and planes of his body against the softer curves and valleys of hers.

When he lifted his mouth, his voice was rough with emotion as he muttered against her lips, "Let's take this inside."

She stared at him, suddenly aware they were about to cross an invisible line.

He swore softly. "Don't look at me like that. Forget the damned feud. For tonight, I'm just Zach. And you're just Jessie. No last names. No family between us."

"Can we do that?" she asked, her voice shaking with confusion while her body pulsed with desire.

"We can do anything we want." He pressed his mouth against the curve of her throat and she closed her eyes, arching to offer him greater access. "Give us tonight, Jessie."

She struggled with her conscience while the

vow she'd made at ten years old to hate all Kerrigans faded beneath the force of her own desire. He'd saved her life tonight. They both could have died if he hadn't acted. *He's not like his uncle and cousin.* This felt like a night out of time, so unusual in all ways that Jessie couldn't bring herself to apply the old rules.

Besides, she wanted this. She wanted *him.*

She fumbled behind her and twisted the doorknob, allowing the door to swing inward. She saw a flare of satisfaction in his eyes before he swung her off her feet and carried her into the apartment.

Jessie woke and stared at the ceiling of her bedroom, disoriented. Then reality flooded back and she realized she was in her own house, in her own room, with Zach's son sleeping down the hall.

It was just a dream. She sat up and kicked her feet free of the tangled sheet so she could swing her legs over the side of the bed. She pushed the heavy mass of hair away from her face. Her temples were damp and she ran her fingertips over her face. They came away wet with tears.

I've got to stop this. He doesn't love me. He

never did. And I don't love him. I'm feeling this way because we had a child together, that's the only reason.

Well, that's one of the biggest lies you've ever told! The small voice resonated inside her skull. Jessie refused to acknowledge it.

Resolutely, she left the bedroom for the shower but the sadness lingered, the memory of the night Zach had shared her bed never far from the surface.

The next morning, she left Rowdy happily puttering with Mr. Harris in his workshop next door while she drove to her parents' home.

"Mom, Dad? Are you home?" she called as she walked down the tiled hallway.

"Back here, Jessie."

She followed the sound of her father's voice and entered the family room, just off the big kitchen. John was reading the Sunday newspaper, glasses perched on his nose, and Margaret was seated on the sofa beside him, the Arts and Entertainment section lying open on her lap.

She set her glass of tea on the table beside her and smiled with pleasure. "Hi, honey, what brings you here so early? Where's Rowdy?"

"He's with Karl Harris—the two of them are cleaning his workshop."

Margaret laughed, her eyes twinkling in appreciation. "By the time they're done, Rowdy will be dirtier than the workshop."

Jessie nodded, managing a smile, and chose a small oak-backed armchair that faced the sofa and her parents. She didn't sit down. Instead, she walked behind it, her hands clasped tightly over the glossy chair back for support. "Are Elizabeth and George here?"

"You just missed them. They left a half hour ago to spend the day with George's sister in town and won't be back until after dinner. Did you need to see them?" Margaret asked.

"No." Jessie was relieved to learn her parents were alone in the house. "I have something I need to talk to you about."

Her parents exchanged a swift, concerned glance, and John removed his reading glasses to focus intently on her.

"What is it, Jessie?" her mother prompted when she paused.

"It's about Rowdy's father." She met her father's gaze. "I lied to you, Dad. I wasn't married to his father and I didn't get a divorce." She winced, wishing she'd said it less bluntly.

"You weren't married?" her father echoed her words, confusion slowly replaced by a frown. "You lied to us? Why?"

"Because I couldn't bring myself to tell you the truth. I made up a fictitious marriage to avoid telling you what really happened."

"A fictitious marriage?" John McCloud's eyes surveyed her with suspicion. His voice measured and tight, he asked, "And what did happen?"

"It's true I met Rowdy's father on campus, but he wasn't a student. He was active military, assigned to the recruiting office." Jessie looked at her mother. Margaret's expression held disbelief and dawning comprehension. "He was standing in line behind me the night the gunman shot up the Starbucks coffee shop. If it hadn't been for his quick thinking in shielding us both behind a display case, I might have been killed. As it was, we both were scratched and bruised by flying debris. Afterward…well, that was the night Rowdy was conceived."

"So my grandson's father is the man who saved your life? Who is he?"

"Zach Kerrigan."

Shock widened her father's eyes before his face flushed and he stood abruptly. "Rowdy's father is a Kerrigan?"

"John!" Margaret rose to stand beside him, clasping his forearm with both hands. "Calm down."

"Calm down? Did you hear what she said?" He glared at her, outraged.

"Yes, I did. And given your reaction, I can certainly see why she didn't want to tell us earlier," Margaret said firmly.

"No wonder the son of a bitch didn't take care of Jessie and the baby," John growled. "He's a Kerrigan."

"He didn't know about Rowdy, Dad. I didn't tell him."

"What? Why not?"

"Because we agreed there couldn't be a future for us. Our families hate each other and I didn't see how we could ever get past what happened to Chase."

"Whether the two of you kept up a connection has no bearing on his obligation to Rowdy. He owes his son support and care. And he owed the same thing to you, damn it." John stalked across the room to the window, then paced back to prop his hands on his hips and glare at her. "A decent man doesn't walk away from his own flesh and blood—nor from the mother of his child. He should have been there when you were carrying Rowdy. Where's he been for the last three years?"

"I didn't tell Zach when I learned I was pregnant. And I didn't tell him about Rowdy when he was born, nor anytime during the years since."

John's jaw actually dropped and he stared at her, clearly stunned. "Why the hell not?"

"Because I didn't think I should, Dad," Jessie snapped. She groaned and dropped onto the chair seat, burying her face in her hands and shaking her head. "If you have to be mad at someone, it should be me. I made a decision that in retrospect may have been a mistake—a serious mistake."

"Don't be so hard on yourself, Jessie," her mother put in. "You were under a lot of pressure to make good grades in law school. The pregnancy had your hormones so unbalanced that half the time you were depressed and the other half you were bouncing off the ceiling. I remember those months very well. Every time I came home

An Important Message from the Editors

Dear Reader,

Because you've chosen to read one of our fine romance novels, we'd like to say "thank you!" And, as a **special** way to thank you, we've selected <u>two more</u> of the books you love so well **plus** two exciting Mystery Gifts to send you— absolutely <u>FREE</u>!

Please enjoy them with our compliments...

Pam Powers

Lift here

Peel off seal and place inside...

How to validate your Editor's
"Thank You"
FREE GIFTS

1. Peel off gift seal from front cover. Place it in space provided at right. This automatically entitles you to receive 2 FREE BOOKS and 2 FREE mystery gifts.

2. Send back this card and you'll get 2 new Silhouette *Special Edition®* novels. These books have a cover price of $4.99 or more each in the U.S. and $5.99 or more each in Canada, but they are yours to keep absolutely free.

3. There's no catch. You're under no obligation to buy anything. We charge nothing—ZERO—for your first shipment. And you don't have to make any minimum number of purchases— not even one!

4. The fact is, thousands of readers enjoy receiving their books by mail from The Silhouette Reader Service™. They enjoy the convenience of home delivery...they like getting the best new novels at discount prices BEFORE they're available in stores... and they love their Reader to Reader subscriber newsletter featuring author news, special book offers, book reviews and much more!

5. We hope that after receiving your free books you'll want to remain a subscriber. But the choice is yours— to continue or cancel, any time at all! So why not take us up on our invitation, with no risk of any kind. You'll be glad you did!

GET TWO *Free* MYSTERY GIFTS...

SURPRISE MYSTERY GIFTS COULD BE YOURS **FREE** AS A SPECIAL "THANK YOU" FROM THE EDITORS

The Editor's "Thank You" Free Gifts Include:

- ○ *Two NEW Romance novels!*
- ○ *Two exciting mystery gifts!*

DETACH AND MAIL CARD TODAY!

Yes! I have placed my

Editor's "Thank You" seal in the
space provided at right. Please
send me 2 free books and
2 free mystery gifts. I
understand I am under no
obligation to purchase any
books, as explained on the
back and on the opposite page.

PLACE
FREE GIFTS
SEAL
HERE

335 SDL EFYR   235 SDL EFXG

FIRST NAME	LAST NAME

ADDRESS

APT.#	CITY

STATE/PROV.	ZIP/POSTAL CODE

(S-SE-08/06)

Thank You!

Offer limited to one per household and not valid to current Silhouette
Special Edition® subscribers.

Your Privacy — Silhouette Books is committed to protecting your privacy. Our Privacy Polic
is available online at www.eharlequin.com or upon request from the Silhouette Reader
Service. From time to time we make our lists of customers available to reputable firms who
may have a product or service of interest to you. If you would prefer for us not to share your
name and address, please check here. ☐

© 2003 HARLEQUIN ENTERPRISES LTD.
® and ™ are trademarks owned and used by the trademark owner and/or its licensee

The Silhouette Reader Service™ — Here's How It Works:

Accepting your 2 free books and 2 free mystery gifts places you under no obligation to buy anything. You may keep the books and gifts and return the shipping statement marked "cancel." If you do not cancel, about a month later we'll send you 6 additional books and bill you just $4.24 each in the U.S., or $4.99 each in Canada, plus 25¢ shipping & handling per book and applicable taxes if any.* That's the complete price and — compared to cover prices starting from $4.99 each in the U.S. and $5.99 each in Canada — it's quite a bargain! You may cancel at any time, but if you choose to continue, every month we'll send you 6 more books, which you may either purchase at the discount price or return to us and cancel your subscription.

*Terms and prices subject to change without notice. Sales tax applicable in N.Y. Canadian residents will be charged applicable provincial taxes and GST. All orders subject to approval. Credit or debit balances in a customer's account(s) may be offset by any other outstanding balance owed by or to the customer. Please allow 4 to 6 weeks for delivery.

If offer card is missing write to: The Silhouette Reader Service, 3010 Walden Ave., P.O. Box 1867, Buffalo, NY 14240-9952

BUSINESS REPLY MAIL
FIRST-CLASS MAIL   PERMIT NO. 717-003   BUFFALO, NY

POSTAGE WILL BE PAID BY ADDRESSEE

SILHOUETTE READER SERVICE
3010 WALDEN AVE
PO BOX 1867
BUFFALO NY 14240-9952

NO POSTAGE
NECESSARY
IF MAILED
IN THE
UNITED STATES

after visiting you at college I told your father I was worried sick about your health."

"It's true," John said, calming down. "She drove herself and everyone else crazy fretting about you."

"That might be an excuse for when I was pregnant," Jessie conceded. "And even for a few months after Rowdy was born. But even I can't stretch it to include all the short years of Rowdy's life."

"And now Kerrigan's back in the county," John said, looking at his only daughter. "What are you going to do about him?"

"I'm going to try and find a way to share my son with his father."

"Do you have to let him see him?" John paused. "Does Kerrigan know?"

"Yes, he knows."

"And how about Rowdy, have you told him?" Margaret asked.

"Not yet. I want to wait until he has time to know Zach better before I tell him." Jessie met her father's gaze. "I wanted to tell you two first so you'll be prepared because he's been asking me lately about why his friends' families are different—the daddy question's bound to come up any day. I'm anticipating he'll be over the moon and beyond excited to claim Zach when he finds out."

"So you're not going to fight to keep Zach away from my grandson?"

"Not if Zach cooperates and not if I'm convinced Rowdy will be happier with his father in his life." Jessie sighed. "I know you'd rather have anyone but a Kerrigan as Rowdy's father, Dad. But unless Zach demonstrates he's hopeless as a father, I won't drag my son through court hearings while Zach and I fight over visitation. I believe the best situation for Rowdy is to have two parents who love him and are ready to work together to give him the best life possible."

"How do you know you can trust a Kerrigan to place Rowdy's interests before his own?"

"I don't," Jessie admitted. "Harlan and Lonnie are unprincipled snakes but until I have proof to the contrary, I have to give Zach the benefit of the doubt and assume he's more like Rachel."

John was obviously unconvinced and started to speak but Margaret intervened. "I think you're being very reasonable and fair, Jessie."

"I'm trying."

"I hope you know what you're doing." John shook his head. "I've got work to do."

The look he gave Jessie before he stalked out of the room left her in no doubt that he was furious with her, but worse, it conveyed a wealth of disappointment.

Determined to face Luke and Rachel next, she left her parents' home and headed to their ranch. Dismay mixed with relief when no one answered her knock on the front door. She stood on the porch, scanning the surrounding corrals and buildings but saw no one.

Giving up, she returned to her vehicle and drove back to town. She'd desperately wanted to tell her entire family about Rowdy and Zach today but Chase had gone to Seattle on a business trip and she had no idea where Luke and Rachel were. Her father hadn't taken her announcement well and she anticipated her conversations with Chase and Luke would be much more difficult. Putting off her confession only gave her more hours to worry about her brothers' reactions.

As the youngest of three children with two older, overly protective brothers, she was accustomed to defending her independence. She wouldn't normally ask for her family's forgiveness or approval of her actions, but this was different. She loved them dearly—and she'd lied to them about her son, the most important thing in her life. So she'd listen if her brothers wanted to stamp and yell, just as long as they didn't take out their anger on Rowdy.

From the beginning, Zach had made it very clear he wanted to openly claim Rowdy as his son as soon as possible. She'd assured him she was telling her entire family this weekend. He'd probably view her failure to tell her brothers as a scheme to delay telling Rowdy the truth.

Ugh, she thought. *Nothing about this situation is going smoothly.*

On Monday, Jessie's business phone rang at half past noon. Alone in the office, she picked up the receiver on the third ring.

"Hello."

"Jessie?"

Zach's deep drawl sent a shiver up her spine and she straightened, the legal brief lying open on her desk forgotten. "Zach. You're back."

"Yeah, just got in. If you haven't eaten yet, I

thought you could meet me for lunch and we could talk about Rowdy."

"I'd like to Zach, but I can't. I have an appointment." She glanced at her watch. "Actually, he was due ten minutes ago."

"How long before you're free?"

"I'm not sure. An hour or so, at least."

"Then I'll grab some lunch and wait. I've got two days of work to catch up on at the ranch and I'd like this settled before I leave town for home."

Jessie heard the hum of voices, faint music and the clatter of crockery in the background. "Do you want to come by the office or should I meet you? Where are you?"

"I'm at the Saloon."

"I can't meet you there." McClouds weren't welcome in the Wolf Creek Saloon. The bar-and-restaurant was owned by the Harper family, and McClouds had been persona non grata in the popular establishment for the last fifteen years. The Harpers had hated the McClouds ever since Chase was convicted of causing Mike Harper's death.

"Okay, then I'll come to your office. Call me when you're finished with your client."

"I'll do that. Bye." Jessie hung up just as the bell on the outer office door to the street jingled.

"Jessie?"

"In here," she called, standing to walk around her desk and into the reception area. "Hello, Bill."

She ushered the middle-aged rancher into her office and was deep in the midst of an explanation of potential tax shelters when the phone rang again. This time, Jessie ignored it, knowing Tina would have returned from lunch and would take a message. But instead, the secretary rapped sharply and partially opened the door to peer around the edge.

"Yes?" Frowning, Jessie looked up. Tina's expression was both apologetic and worried. "What is it?"

"I'm sorry to interrupt you, Jessie, but I think you might want to take this call. It's your mother." Tina beckoned urgently, silently conveying a wish for Jessie to take the call in the front office.

Jessie smiled calmly at her client. "Excuse me a moment, Bill. I'm sure this won't take long. You might want to look at this spreadsheet while I'm gone." She slid a comparison sheet for several tax shelters across the desk and stood, crossing the room to join Tina. She stepped outside and closed the door quietly behind her. "Tina, what on earth…"

"Your mom's really upset—you'd better talk to her." Tina lifted the receiver on her desk phone and handed it to Jessie before turning off her headset.

"Hi, Mom. What's wrong?"

"Jessie, thank goodness I caught you." Margaret's anxiety was clear. "Your dad just got home. Chase is back from Seattle and rode out to the west pasture where John was working. Your dad told him about Zach being Rowdy's father. He said Chase didn't say much but he left almost immediately. I'm afraid he's looking for Zach. I called his ranch but no one answered so I tried Rachel, who told me Zach's out of town, but she thought he was coming home today."

"He's home." Jessie thought quickly. "How long ago did Chase leave?"

"John said it was about forty minutes."

"Thanks for the heads-up, Mom. I'll try to stop Chase before he finds Zach."

"I hope you do," Margaret said fervently. "Your dad's on his way into town but Chase has a head start and I doubt John can catch him in time. I don't want Chase in jail for assault and you know how he feels about you raising Rowdy alone."

"Yes, Mom, I do. I have to go. I'll call you as soon as I know anything." Jessie didn't wait to hear her mother say goodbye. She dropped the phone and headed for the door. "Tina, apologize to Bill for me and reschedule him."

"Sure—where are you going?" Tina called after her as Jessie yanked open the door and left the office.

The Wolf Creek Saloon was four blocks away. Jessie moved quickly, dodging a group of shoppers in front of Dougan's Pharmacy.

She scanned the cars and pickups slotted into parking spaces and jerked to a stop when she reached a dark-green pickup with the distinctive McCloud Ranch logo on the driver's door. The truck was parked directly in front of McGonagle's Feed Store. Jessie went inside but she didn't see Chase.

"Hey, Jessie." Mack McGonagle walked down the aisle toward her, the worn floorboards creaking under his boots. "What brings you in?"

"I'm looking for Chase. Have you seen him?"

"Yeah, he was here a few minutes ago."

"Do you know where he went?"

"Well, I'm guessing he went over to the Saloon. He asked me if I'd seen Zach Kerrigan. I told him I was sweeping the sidewalk out front when Zach parked in front of the Saloon and went inside about an hour ago. Hey," he yelled after her when she turned and ran out. "What's goin' on?"

Jessie didn't reply. She was still three blocks from the Saloon and Chase was nowhere in sight. Which probably meant he'd already gone inside.

"Damn," she muttered. Heat bounced off the sidewalk in waves. The fine shell she wore beneath her pale lemon suit clung to her heated skin. She wished she was wearing jogging shoes instead of her chic strappy sandals with their three-inch heels. She hiked her narrow-cut skirt higher on her thighs and started running.

Chapter Six

Zach glanced at his wristwatch and lifted his glass. He'd drained the last drop of cold tea at least fifteen minutes ago and only ice cubes remained. Too impatient to let the chunk of ice melt in his mouth, he crunched it, swallowed and shook another piece into his mouth.

Jessie said she'd be finished in an hour. He looked at his watch again and drummed his fingers. The minutes crawled by. He'd been away from the ranch for two days and knew a mountain of work waited for him, but he didn't want to leave town for the ranch without talking to Jessie.

"Want a refill, Zach?" the bartender asked, lifting a sweat-beaded pitcher filled with tea.

"No, thanks." Zach glanced around the bar. The restaurant next door had been full when he'd arrived. The Saloon made room for the overflow crowd at its booths and tables and Zach had claimed a stool at the long bar. The noisy lunch crowd had started leaving just before 1:00 p.m. Now only Zach, the bartender and three ranchers seated in a back booth were left in the big air-conditioned room.

The door to the sidewalk opened behind him. Zach glanced into the mirror, stiffening, his eyes assessing the reflection of the man who entered and halted just inside the door.

Chase McCloud's gaze met his. Zach turned and stood, facing him. Jessie's brother radiated menace. Zach didn't have to ask if he'd heard about Rowdy.

"Kerrigan." The single word held a lethal threat.

"McCloud." Zach's voice carried the same ice.

Chase moved toward him, stopping barely five

feet away. Zach stepped away from the bar, muscles tensed.

"I've been looking forward to this for almost four years."

"Yeah?" Zach shifted, widening his stance, his hands curling into loose fists.

The door slammed open with a bang. Neither man looked around.

"Chase!" Jessie hurried across the scuffed wood floor and caught her brother's arm. "What are you doing?"

"Go home, Jessie." Chase didn't look at her. All his attention was focused on Zach.

"Please, Chase. Don't do this." Her voice was pitched low, throaty with urgency. "I know what you're thinking, but you're wrong."

"No. I'm not."

"Stop being so stubborn." She wrapped both hands around his forearm and shook him. "I don't know what Dad told you but you obviously didn't hear the whole story." The jukebox in the far corner played the last bar of Johnny Cash's "I Walk The Line" and the room went suddenly silent. "This is my fault, not Zach's."

The three men in the back booth and the bartender had all been watching the confrontation. Jessie's last words echoed in the quiet room and made them abandon any pretense of disinterest. All four of them stared at Jessie and her brother, then at Zach.

"For God's sake, Jessie," Chase growled, glaring blackly at their audience. "Go home."

"No." She stepped between the two men, her back to Zach while she faced Chase. "This isn't your problem. It's mine. And I'll deal with it."

"You're my sister. *I'll* deal with it. Now get out of my way." Chase's hand lifted.

Zach moved with lightning speed, shifting Jessie behind him to shield her from her brother.

"You lay a hand on her and you're dead."

Chase froze, his eyes flaring with surprise before they narrowed. "You must have me confused with your uncle and cousin, Kerrigan. I don't hit women."

"That's good. Because you'd have to go through me first." Behind him, Jessie's startled silence ended with an exasperated huff of sound and she pushed at his arm. He reached behind him to hold her still and his hand found the curve of her waist. She immediately shoved it away.

Chase stared at him for a long, silent moment, then looked at Jessie, struggling to move past Zach. "What part of this didn't Dad tell me?" he asked.

"I'm not telling you in front of half of Wolf Creek," she snapped. "For once in your life, stop acting like an overprotective Neanderthal and just go home. I promise I'll tell you everything later."

Chase swept his gaze over the big, nearly empty room. "Half of Wolf Creek?" Amusement colored his voice. "You tend to exaggerate, Jessie-girl." He looked at Zach and his face was at once hostile, his eyes cold. "Step outside in the alley, Kerrigan, and we'll settle this."

Zach shifted to move toward the door and Jessie locked her arms around his waist. "No!"

He twisted to make eye contact with her. She was pressed against his back, her breasts crushed against him, and she looked mad enough to spit.

"I swear, if you two don't stop this, I'll never forgive either one of you."

"This is inevitable, Jessie," he muttered. "Give it up. Let go of me." He was reluctant to forcibly put her away from him and he suspected she knew it.

"If it's inevitable, then it doesn't matter if you both wait until I've talked to Chase," she shot back.

"That's up to your brother." Zach looked at Chase. "Your call, McCloud."

"Hell." Chase growled. "You're a pain in the ass, Jessie. We'll take this up again in private after she 'explains,' Kerrigan."

"Anytime."

Chase nodded curtly and turned on his heel. He brushed past a slender woman dressed in jeans and a white T-shirt with Wolf Creek Saloon stamped on the front, muttering a brief apology before he shoved open the door and disappeared.

The woman's eyes widened. She stopped, turning to stare after Chase. When the door closed, she looked over her shoulder at Zach.

"Wasn't that Chase McCloud? What was he doing in here, Zach?"

Still half-concealed behind him, Jessie's fingers tightened on his arm. Zach gave her a reassuring squeeze. "He was looking for me, Raine."

"Then I guess I should be relieved my bar isn't trashed," Raine Harper said wryly as she walked toward them. Her smile faded and she stiffened

when Jessie stepped to the side, out from behind
Zach's protection. "Well, I see the big bad bounty
hunter isn't the only McCloud on Harper property." Her voice was even, lacking the warm friend-
liness it had held when she spoke to Zach.

"I was just leaving." Jessie was equally polite,
and equally wary.

Zach caught her arm, staying her while he
pulled a handful of bills out of his pocket and
dropped several on the polished bar. He nodded
to the bartender, settled his Stetson more firmly
on his head, and still holding Jessie's arm, walked
her to the door.

"See you, Raine." He touched the brim of his
hat as they passed.

"Zach," the woman acknowledged, her expression openly curious as her gaze flicked over them.

His hand firmly clasped around Jessie's upper
arm, Zach took her with him out of the saloon and
across the sidewalk to his truck. He pulled open
the passenger door, caught Jessie by the waist and
lifted her inside. Ignoring her startled gasp, he
stepped back and slammed the door before she
could protest.

He circled the truck and slid behind the wheel,

turned the ignition key and threw the vehicle into reverse. "Fasten your seat belt." He backed out of the parking space without waiting for Jessie to comply.

"Where are we going?" she asked.

"Somewhere quiet and less public where we can talk without an audience." He braked and turned left at the end of the block. Within moments, he parked the truck in her driveway and got out. She was just climbing out of the passenger seat when he reached her.

The four-wheel drive truck cab was higher than a car chassis. Jessie's skirt inched up her legs as she eased off the leather seat and slid toward the ground.

Zach caught her just before her toes touched the drive. She wobbled on her high heels, grabbing his arms for balance. With swift reflexes he wrapped his arms around her, supporting her with his body. She was pressed against him, her slim thighs aligned with his, the soft weight of her breasts crushed against his chest.

They both froze.

Her hair brushed the underside of his chin and throat, the silky mane releasing the seductive fragrance that was uniquely Jessie. He was instantly hit with a wave of lust, longing and vivid memories of holding her during their one night together. For an insane moment, he couldn't think beyond carrying her into the house and laying her down on the nearest flat surface. Then she eased back, putting inches between them. Her scent still filled his lungs but her soft weight no longer made his body go crazy and his brain refuse to function.

"You all right?" His voice rasped, husky with his struggle for control.

"Yes." She pushed her hair away from her face with unsteady fingers and a flush of heat bloomed over the curve of her cheeks. She tugged on the hem of her jacket, straightening it before she ran her hands over the pale yellow fabric covering her thighs, smoothing away nonexistent wrinkles. "Let's go inside."

Zach nodded and followed her down the short sidewalk to her porch. *If I have to want her, it's good to know it's mutual. Even if neither of us is willing to do anything about it.*

Jessie lifted a pot filled with bright red geraniums from the wicker table to the left of the door and took a brass key from beneath the terra-cotta.

Zach shook his head. "That's the best place you could think of to hide your spare key? Under a flowerpot?"

"I know it's obvious but Wolf Creek isn't a hotbed of home burglaries. I'm not worried." She unlocked the door and went inside.

Zach stepped into the living room, letting the screen door slap gently shut behind him. Jessie moved ahead of him, turning to face him only when the width of the room separated them.

"I'm sorry my brother confronted you, Zach. I told my parents the truth about you and Rowdy on the weekend but Chase was in Seattle. And Luke wasn't home, either—I think he took Rachel to Billings for the weekend."

"So Luke doesn't know I'm Rowdy's father?"

"No. Not unless Mom or Dad told him," she amended. "That's how Chase found out—he saw Dad today."

"How did your parents take the news?" Zach asked.

"About as I expected. Mom was reasonable and Dad exploded." She folded her arms in an unconsciously protective gesture.

"Exploded? You mean he was angry or do you

mean he hit something?" Zach's real concern was whether John McCloud had been violent with Jessie but he tempered his question.

"I meant he was angry, of course." She frowned at him. "My Dad couldn't bring himself to spank me when I was a child and misbehaved. The possibility of him hitting me now that I'm an adult is inconceivable. I'm sure it would never occur to him. And while we're on the subject," she added, planting her hands on her hips. "There is *no* way either of my brothers would hit a woman, either. That *is* what you thought back at the Saloon, isn't it? That Chase was going to hit me?"

"It occurred to me," Zach agreed. "Maybe not on purpose, but I didn't want you catching a fist meant for me."

"I hardly think Chase would have mistaken me for you if he started swinging. Would you have?"

"No. But that's different."

"How is it different?" Her dark brows winged upward in disbelief.

"It just is," Zach growled, refusing to confess he'd instinctively shifted her behind him because he felt protective and possessive. He felt the same way about his mother and sister but had always chalked it up to being the only man in the family after his father died. It was his nature to defend what he claimed as his own. He doubted Jessie would accept that he'd stepped between her and Chase because he felt she belonged to him. He gave her an edited version. "Your brother has a reputation for being a damn good bounty hunter and violence is part of the job description. I didn't want you standing between us. You could have been hurt accidentally."

"My brother would never hit me, even accidentally." Her voice rang with conviction.

"If you say so." Zach shrugged and purposely changed the subject. "It's pretty clear your family isn't happy about the situation but as far as I'm concerned, that doesn't change our agreement. I want to spend time with Rowdy and I want us to tell him he's my son as soon as possible."

"As you said, our agreement hasn't changed," she challenged him. "I want him to know you better before he learns you're his father."

Zach had expected Jessie would refuse to budge on this point but thought it had been worth a try. "Then let's work out a schedule for visits. The more time we spend together, the better he'll know me and the sooner he can be told he's my son."

"All right…" Jessie headed toward the kitchen. "We can use the calendar in here."

Zach followed her. Jessie took a large Monet print calendar from the wall next to the refrigerator, found a pen in the drawer beneath and they sat down at the table with the calendar between them. A half hour later the blank squares for the next two weeks were nearly filled with jotted notes, starting with a visit to Zach's ranch the following Saturday.

Zach left for his ranch and the long list of work waiting for him while Jessie donned tennis shoes, tucked her heels into a canvas tote bag and headed downtown to her office. She reached the end of her residential street before she realized she'd neglected to ask Zach an important question. With her cell phone tucked inside her purse at her office, she was forced to wait until she reached her desk to call him. His answering machine picked up on the fifth ring.

"Zach, this is Jessie. I forgot to ask if you've told your mother and Rachel. If you've talked to them, did you warn them not to say anything to

Rowdy? Could you leave a message for me on my home phone and let me know? Thanks."

She hung up and slumped in her chair.

Life is getting too complicated. She was sure Tina hadn't believed her brief, evasive explanation about why she'd left the office so abruptly. And the local gossips were sure to have a field day with the story of her running down Main Street in the midday heat to stop a fight between her brother and Zach.

And then there were those brief moments when she'd nearly stumbled getting out of Zach's truck and he'd caught her, holding her safe and close. The scent of his faintly spicy aftershave, the flex and shift of hard muscles against hers, the strength of the arms that held her—the memory had the power to shake her even now.

Jessie determinedly shelved the unwelcome feeling of vulnerability and squared her shoulders, opening a file on her desk and immersing herself in work.

Jessie arrived home from work to find a message from Zach on her answering machine. His brief assurance that he hadn't discussed Rowdy with his mother or Rachel was a relief. However, now that her parents and Chase knew, Jessie was convinced it was only a matter of time, probably very little time, before someone told Luke. And Luke would tell Rachel. Rachel would certainly tell her mother and both of them would demand explanations.

The second message was from Chase, telling her he'd see her later that evening.

She was waiting when he drove up just after 9:00 p.m. and held the screen door open for him as he climbed the porch steps.

"Let's go in the kitchen." She led the way and he followed. She was reminded of the night Zach had walked behind her into the kitchen and was struck by the similarities between the two tall, menacing men.

Of all the people she had to confront with her news, this was the hardest. She leaned against the counter and faced him. She adored her brother. Never before now had he looked at her with the remote, cold stare he used with the world outside their family. It was impossible to tell just how angry he was.

"You said you wanted to explain what happened with Kerrigan."

"Yes." Jessie drew a deep breath and began.

When she stopped speaking, Chase just stared at her, his expression enigmatic.

"Let me make sure I've got this straight. Kerrigan saved your life in Missoula after which the two of you spent the night together. He left the country and you never told him you were pregnant. You didn't tell him until almost four years later when he came home and saw Rowdy. In the meantime, you lied to Mom and Dad, and Luke and me, about being married to keep us from looking for Rowdy's real father. Is that right?"

"Unfortunately, yes."

"And now you're trying to untangle this mess and you want Luke, Dad and me to stay away from Kerrigan?"

"Yes."

"Hell." Chase shook his head in disgust. "Is this whole family going insane? First Luke falls in love with Rachel and now you've had a kid with a Kerrigan? Am I the only one that thinks this is damned odd?"

"No, you're not." Jessie was so relieved his cold rage had been replaced with disgruntlement that she was willing to agree to anything.

"The folks are probably glad Rachel and Zach don't have another sister."

"Why?"

"Because she'd probably be stalking me, looking for a husband," Chase said dryly.

Jessie burst out laughing. The relief of knowing Chase wasn't angry at her was enormous. But the laughter turned to tears.

"Hey." Alarmed, Chase pulled her into his arms and patted her back. "What did I say?"

"You're not mad," she got out.

"Not at you. Kerrigan—now that's different."

She tipped her head back and looked up at him. His eyes had an icy glint and her heart sank.

"Please tell me you aren't going to fight with him, Chase."

"I haven't decided."

He refused to be more forthcoming and she had to be satisfied with his answer. He shared chocolate cake and coffee with her and they chatted about other topics until he left around eleven o'clock.

Jessie went to bed no closer to knowing how Chase felt about Zach and whether her brother intended to remain neutral.

* * *

By the weekend, she still hadn't heard from Luke and she was exhausted from bracing herself for the confrontation with Zach's mother and sister that hadn't materialized.

She bundled Rowdy into her SUV and drove to Zach's ranch on Saturday morning because the note on her kitchen calendar read "Zach's place." She'd never before set foot on Kerrigan land and hoped her childhood conviction—that lightning would immediately strike her if she did—was only a little girl's fear.

Zach lived on Section Ten of what had once been the Kerrigan Conglomerate. The cluster of ranch buildings had been left to Rachel by their grandfather, Marcus, but Rachel moved to Luke's home after their marriage, leaving Section Ten empty. Zach, Rachel and their mother, Judith, had officially joined their inherited acres in a partnership headed by Zach. He'd taken over Section Ten buildings and made it the official headquarters of the new JRZ Ranch.

"How come we're visiting Uncle Zach, Mommy?" Rowdy asked as she parked in front of the two-story ranch house and switched off the engine.

"Because he invited us," she answered calmly as she left her seat and opened Rowdy's door.

"Is he your friend?"

Now there's a loaded question. "He's a very nice man," she said evasively.

"Does he have horses like Grandpa John?"

"I'm sure he has horses, maybe not as many as Grandpa, though." Jessie released his safety harness. The little boy immediately jumped out of his car seat and clambered out onto the gravel.

Jessie turned in a half circle, looking for Zach. The dusty ranch yard and buildings seemed empty, except for horses grazing in a pasture beyond the barns. The sturdy, old-fashioned barn had new shingles on the red roof and replacement poles in the adjoining corral, where stalks of pale gold color interspersed with the older, weathered gray wood. A recent addition, the long horse barn gleamed with fresh paint on the far side. Rachel's million-dollar quarter horse stud, Ransom, lived here on Section Ten and the money he earned was apparently being put to good use.

The sun's rays burned, unfiltered by a single white cloud in the deep blue sky. Jessie plopped a Mariner's ball cap on Rowdy's head to protect

him from the heat and leaned into the backseat of
the SUV to retrieve a bottle of water.

"Hi, Uncle Zach!"

She glanced over her shoulder. Zach strode toward them from the barn, his long legs eating up
the distance in no time. Rowdy ran toward him
and he grinned, pausing to listen when the three-
year-old skidded to a stop in front of him.

Jessie closed the SUV's door and waited for the
two to reach her. Zach wore a white T-shirt tucked
into worn Levi's, scuffed black cowboy boots and
a straw cowboy hat. The soft white cotton shirt
and faded denim jeans faithfully outlined the powerful muscles of a body she remembered only too
well.

Rowdy hopped and ran to keep up with Zach's
longer stride as they drew nearer. "Mommy said
you have horses. Can we see your horses?"

"Sure. You can feed them, too."

"Wow." Rowdy beamed up at him. They
reached Jessie and he grabbed her hand. "We're
going to feed the horses. Hurry."

Jessie laughed. "Slow down, kiddo. I'm sure
Zach will wait for us."

"But I want to see them now." He turned to look

up at Zach. "Do you have any little horses like my Aunt Rachel's? She has one that's almost my size."

"No, son, I don't have miniature horses. But there's something little in the barn you might like," Zach added.

Jessie froze and felt her eyes widen in shock. A quick search of Zach's features led her to believe he hadn't registered the significance of his calling Rowdy "son." She looked at Rowdy but his face held only bright interest. She drew a deep breath and concentrated on Rowdy's response.

"What?"

"I think I'll let you find out for yourself. Do you want to feed the horses first, or check out the surprise in the barn?"

"The surprise first," Rowdy said promptly.

The barn interior was dim, dust motes dancing in the shafts of sunlight that stole their way in through small cracks in the siding. Zach led the way down the center aisle and stopped at a stall near the far end.

"Here they are." He swung open the gate and stepped inside. "Hey, Zarina," he crooned, kneeling on the thick layer of clean straw. "Easy, girl. It's all right. These are friends of mine."

Jessie and Rowdy peered around Zach. An Australian sheep dog lay on her side and puppies tumbled, climbed and rolled playfully over and around her. She whined anxiously and Zach smoothed his palm over her head, calming her. He glanced over his shoulder. "Would you like to hold one of her puppies, Rowdy?"

"Yes." He nodded, eyes rounded with delight.

Zach picked up a puppy and beckoned him closer. "Sit down, son."

Rowdy obediently dropped to sit cross-legged on the straw. Zach carefully placed the fat little black-and-white fur ball in his arms and the puppy wriggled, licking Rowdy's face and chin with his pink tongue.

The other puppies left their mother's side to climb over Rowdy's legs. One of them pattered across the straw to sniff at Jessie's sandal. Charmed, she picked him up, the chubby little body warm and sweet.

"Aren't you just the cutest thing," she said, laughing as the puppy licked her hand and woofed, eyeing her expectantly. Then he planted one paw on her collarbone before slipping, dragging the neckline of her tank top lower until the lace of her white bra was visible. "Hey!" She caught his paw and tugged it and the pink cotton upward. The puppy squirmed and tried to lick her chin. She tilted her head back to avoid the little tongue and was snared by Zach's hot stare.

The air was suddenly much too thick, too heated to breathe. Jessie's body reacted instantly to the sexual awareness throbbing between them.

"Can we take this one home, Mommy?" Rowdy asked, squeezing his puppy with enthusiasm. The pup yipped, wiggling with energy, and Rowdy instantly loosened his grip.

His innocent question broke the tension that held them and Jessie mouthed "no" at Zach while Rowdy was busy juggling the squirming puppy.

"That depends," Zach told him. "They're too young to leave their mother so you have a few weeks to let your mom think about it."

"Can I have this one? Please, Mommy?" Rowdy's face was hopeful, his eyes pleading with her.

"We'll see," Jessie replied.

"Good mornin'."

Jessie looked over her shoulder and smiled. Charlie Ankrum had worked for the Kerrigan family for as long as Jessie could remember. He'd somehow managed to remain neutral and not take sides in the long-standing feud. "Hello, Charlie."

He entered the box stall and joined them, gnarled hands propped on his lean hips as he looked down at the mother dog with her puppies scrambling over Rowdy's legs in the straw. "And who might you be, young man?"

"This is Rowdy," Jessie replied. "Rowdy, say hello to Mr. Ankrum."

"Hi, Mr. Ankrum," Rowdy said politely before returning his attention to the puppy who was now chewing on his belt.

"Nice to meet you, Rowdy." Charlie chuckled at the sight of one little boy trying to control several rambunctious puppies. "Call me Charlie."

"Okay." Rowdy grinned.

"I haven't seen you in town in ages, Charlie," Jessie said. "How have you been?"

"Not too bad, considerin' my age." Charlie gestured at his left leg. "I have to have some minor surgery on my bum knee before long, but other than that, I'm healthy. No need to ask how you are—you're as pretty as ever." He winked at her. "How are your folks?"

"They're well. Dad bought a new plane."

"I heard Jack Macomber was trying to talk him into buying his crop duster."

"Yes," Jessie said. "He succeeded. I think Mom's worried he'll try stunt flying with it."

Charlie laughed. "She's probably right to worry. John just might do that." He turned to Zach. "I stopped to tell you I'm runnin' into town to pick up the pump replacement parts we ordered. Anything you want me to get for you?"

"Not that I can think of," Zach said.

"Then I'll take off." He nodded to Jessie and touched the brim of his straw Resistol in an old-fashioned gesture. "Sure nice to see you, Jessie. And nice to meet you, young man."

Rowdy copied the salute, bumping the bill of his Mariner's hat and knocking it askew. "'Bye."

The adults laughed and Charlie left.

Two hours later, stuffed with lunch followed by ice cream, Jessie and Rowdy drove away from the ranch. Rowdy chattered about the puppies all the way home while Jessie murmured noncommittal responses.

She couldn't forget that moment in the stall when she looked up and found Zach watching her. He still wanted her. What was she going to do about it?

* * *

Zach lay flat on his back under a 1955 Chevy truck just outside the open doors of the machine shop. The old flatbed vehicle's stubborn bolts made changing its oil and greasing it a challenge. He'd been at it for over an hour when he heard the growl of a diesel engine growing steadily louder. He twisted sideways, grunting when he rolled over a rock that dug into his shoulder, and lifted his head off the concrete to look past the truck's undercarriage and down the gravel lane.

A black pickup drove into the ranch yard, stopped near the house, then continued on to the machine shop and parked.

Zach slid out from beneath the truck and got to his feet, wiping the grease and oil from his hands with a red mechanics rag.

When he saw John McCloud shove open the driver's door and step out, Zach went still, then slowly finished wiping his hands before tucking the grease-streaked rag into his back pocket.

"Mr. McCloud," he said politely, his tone carefully neutral while he braced himself, wondering if Jessie's father had come to finish what Chase had started at the saloon. John McCloud was an older version of his two sons, just as big, just as work-hardened, and from all accounts, just as tough.

"Kerrigan." His voice was equally neutral.

"What can I do for you?"

"I want to talk to you about my daughter and grandson."

"All right." Zach waited, his gaze unwavering.

"Jessie made me promise I wouldn't interfere in what's between you two. But just so we're clear, if you hurt my little girl or my grandson, you'll answer to me."

Anger flared, bright and hot. Zach forced his fists to uncurl. "If you were anyone else but Jessie's father," he said evenly, "this conversation would be over. But given the circumstances, I guess you're entitled."

"Huh," John grunted, his gaze sharpening. "Jessie claims you didn't know about Rowdy until last week. Is that true?"

"It's true."

John shoved his hands in his jeans pockets. "I can't say I think she did the right thing, not telling you. But I sure as hell don't understand why you didn't check on her and find out for yourself."

"I flew back to the States to see her. When I heard she was married, I figured we didn't have anything to talk about so I went back to Afghanistan without seeing her."

"Is that right?" John said, clearly surprised. "Well I'll be damned. And she never was married. What a mess."

Stunned, Zach stared at him. "What do you mean, she wasn't married?"

"I mean she never had a husband. She told us she made up the story so her brothers and me wouldn't go looking for Rowdy's father. Looking for you," he amended. "Doesn't make a hell of a lot of sense, does it?"

"She wasn't married," Zach muttered, shock slowly giving way to fierce satisfaction that Jessie hadn't been married and growing anger that she'd lied to him.

"No." John's eyes narrowed. "And her mother tells me Jessie hasn't dated anyone since before Rowdy was born."

Zach didn't comment. He could read the suspicion on the older man's face but he wouldn't speculate as to why Jessie hadn't dated anyone since their night together. He had lots of questions but he wasn't about to ask John McCloud for answers. Jessie, however, had some explaining to do.

"Well, then…" John settled his Stetson more firmly on his head. "I've said what I came here to say." He nodded in curt farewell, turned and climbed back into his truck.

Zach watched the cloud of dust roll up behind the pickup's wheels as it tooled down the lane.

"Damn," he said aloud, staring at the empty road. "She wasn't married."

He glanced at his watch. Jessie was probably still at work and it would be several hours before she tucked Rowdy into bed for the night. He had time to finish changing the oil in the old truck before showering and driving into Wolf Creek. He had questions and this time, he thought grimly, Jessie better give him straight answers.

Jessie waited until Rowdy was fast asleep before shaking bath salts into the tub and filling it with water. The half hour she spent relaxing in the warm, jasmine-scented bath eased the tension from her body, loosening muscles that felt perennially tense since Zach's return. When she left the bathroom, the ends of her ponytail and the tendrils at her nape were damp and curling from the steamy air.

She padded down the hall, her feet bare below her favorite cotton pajama pants. The frosted pink polish on her toenails was the exact shade of the chrysanthemums splashed across the fabric and the satin ribbon edging the hems. She'd smoothed on lotion after her bath and the light yellow tank top and matching, loose floral bottoms were cool and soft against her bare skin.

The refrigerator held both iced tea and bottled water. She chose cold water and sat at the table, taking a file from her briefcase and opening it. A knock on the door interrupted her before she could flip open the manila folder. A quick glance at the wall clock above the refrigerator confirmed the time was 9:10 p.m.

"What in the world?" she murmured as she rose. Through the window of the darkened living room, she saw the shadowy shape of a man standing on her porch, tall, broad and so distinctive she immediately knew his identity. "Zach?" She unlocked the screen door and pushed it open. "I didn't know you were coming in to see Rowdy to-night. I'm sorry, but he's already asleep."

He stepped inside. "I'm not here to see Rowdy."

"You're not?" Nonplussed, she tried to read his expression, but failed.

"Where can we talk without Rowdy overhearing us?" he asked.

"Here in the living room is fine. I need to close the door to his bedroom—I'll only be a minute." Jessie moved quietly down the hallway, peering in to find Rowdy sprawled across the bed, asleep amid his stuffed animals. She eased the door closed and returned to the living room, pausing to switch on a small lamp next to the sofa. "What is it, Zach? Is something wrong?"

"Your dad came to see me this afternoon."

"Oh, no," Jessie groaned. "I'm so sorry." She scanned his face for bruises but found none. *Maybe they didn't fight.* "He didn't try to punch you or anything, did he? Please tell me he didn't."

"No, he didn't. But we had an interesting conversation."

"Really?" There was something more, Jessie knew. She could sense it in the edginess beneath the deliberately even tone of his words. "What did you talk about?"

"Your marriage. He says there wasn't one."

Jessie froze. It hadn't occurred to her that anyone in her family would tell Zach about her fictitious husband before she had a chance to do so. She'd been worried her father or brothers might confront him and exchange blows, but the possibility they might carry on an actual conversation hadn't crossed her mind. *What were the odds?*

"Dad's right. I wasn't married."

"Maybe you'd like to explain why you forgot to mention that little detail?" Fury simmered beneath his words. "It's not as if the subject of your marriage hasn't come up."

"I know," she acknowledged.

"So. Explain. I'd like to hear the story you told your parents."

"Dad didn't tell you?"

"I didn't ask him. I wanted to hear it from you."

"I would have told you, sooner or later," she began.

The look he gave her was filled with disbelief. He didn't speak, waiting pointedly for her to continue.

"First, you have to understand my father and brothers are extremely protective of me—beyond protective, actually. I often think they're downright irrational. When I learned I was pregnant, my first instinct was to call my parents but I knew if I did, my dad would demand to know who the father was, and where he was. If I'd told him you were my baby's father and that you'd left the States, he would have moved heaven and earth to track you down. He'd have contacted your commanding officer and who knows what kind of trouble he might have caused for you."

"At least I would have known you were pregnant."

Jessie winced. "Yes. And we both know you wouldn't have welcomed the news."

"What the hell makes you say that?"

"Surely you're not claiming you'd have been happy to find out I was expecting a baby, Zach? We both thought we'd never see each other again when you left my apartment that morning in Missoula. It was pretty clear you didn't *want* to see me. The last person in the world you'd have wanted to hear that news from was me." Jessie searched his features but read only leashed rage in his shadowed eyes and taut jawline, where a muscle flexed sporadically. She saw no indication that he agreed with her.

"So you decided I shouldn't be told?" He bit off an oath. "The truth is you didn't want me to know, Jessie. If you didn't tell me, you wouldn't have to deal with a Kerrigan and you wouldn't have to share Rowdy."

"That's not true." Jessie crossed her arms over her midriff in an unconsciously protective gesture. "I would have told you, Zach."

"When?" he shot back.

"When you came back to Wolf Creek, when you lived close enough to have a relationship with Rowdy and see him on a regular basis."

"And what did you think the odds were I would ever have come back here? If my grandfather hadn't split the Kerrigan holdings and left me land, I might not have. You know that. And then you would never have had to tell me. Tell me, Jessie, would you have relented and sent me a picture when he graduated high school? College, maybe? Would you have invited me to his wedding? Just when would I have found out I had a son? When it was too late for me to know him?"

"I'm not saying I made the right decision, Zach, nor even that I made a *good* decision. I can only tell you I did the best I could under the circumstances."

"Yeah, well, what you did was wrong. And it wasn't the best you could have done." He stalked toward her, not stopping until he loomed over her and she had to tilt her head backward to meet his gaze. "The best you could have done was to have told me."

"You were thousands of miles away," she protested, throwing up her hands in frustration. "What would have been different?"

His eyes flared. "If I'd known you were carrying my baby I'd have come home and claimed you both." He reached for her, dragging her against him and covering her mouth with his.

His mouth took hers with angry impatience and his arms wrapped her tight against the hardness of his body. For a moment, she was stunned by the surge of heat but then she struggled in protest, pushing against his chest.

Instantly, his mouth gentled over hers, his hold loosening just enough to keep her body touching his. She would have fought restraint but she had no defense against the slow seduction of his mouth luring hers and the heat of his body surrounding her.

Yes. Her body followed her heart, going boneless against his as she reached for him, sliding her fingers through the cool strands of his hair.

He picked her up and she instinctively wrapped her legs around his waist and her arms around his neck. The soft cotton tank top rode up, baring her midriff and Zach groaned, tearing his mouth from hers, his breathing labored.

"You're naked under this, aren't you."

It wasn't a question. His voice was tortured.

She nodded, her lips seeking his and he groaned again.

Her heart slammed against her ribs as their mouths fed off each other with feverish intensity. At last he tore himself from her and met her gaze, his eyes hot.

"You and that damned stupid story about being married," he muttered. "We've wasted years." He turned in a half circle. "Where's your bedroom?"

Dazed, Jessie opened her mouth to tell him and at that second, her sleeping conscience chose to wake and shriek a warning.

"Wait!"

"Why? What's wrong?" His voice was distracted, husky with arousal.

"We can't do this."

His expression was incredulous. "You're kidding, right?" He moved his hips beneath hers and she gasped. "It feels to me like we definitely can do this."

"Stop that." She battled a rush of heated desire and pushed at his shoulders. "Put me down."

Reluctantly, he let her unwind her legs from around his waist to slide down his body. His breath hissed out and she gasped audibly when her thighs and the cove of her hips moved over his.

"So what's wrong?" he asked, his voice tight with restraint.

"This, us." She gestured wildly, waving a hand at him, then herself. "We can't do this. It's not good."

"It felt pretty damned good to me."

"That's not what I meant and you know it." She pushed her tumbled mane of hair, minus the fabric scrunchie that had somehow become lost in the last frantic moments, away from her face. "Giving in to lust and hormones four years ago is how we ended up in this predicament."

"Don't knock lust and hormones," he growled. "People all over the world would kill for the amount of lust we've got going for us."

She hadn't expected or wanted him to deny the heat between them, but his easy agreement seemed to confirm lust was all he felt for her and that made her feel like crying. "Yes, well…" She drew in a deep, shaky breath and lifted her chin. "We still don't have solutions for what happened the last time we gave in to lust. And since I'm not on birth control, I don't think it's wise to repeat ourselves."

"You're not on birth control? Why, Jessie?"

His voice was curious, interested. But Jessie wasn't fooled. *Dumb, Jessie, very dumb. Why did you tell him?* "My practicing birth control, or not, is none of your business, Zach."

"It is now," he said. "So tell me, why is a young, beautiful, single woman like you not taking birth control?"

"I haven't felt I needed to," she said tightly.

"How long since you 'felt the need to'?"

"I don't see why that's relevant."

"But I do." He leaned closer, his eyes searching hers. "Have you slept with anyone since Rowdy was born?"

"It's none of your business," she ground out. She refused to give him the satisfaction of hearing her admit he'd been her last lover.

"Then I'm going to assume you haven't."

"Assume what you like," she responded, feeling her cheeks burn at the note of male satisfaction in his voice. "It has no bearing on the present situation. We need to stay focused on resolving the issues surrounding Rowdy."

Her brisk voice was the one she used in the courtroom. Instead of being annoyed with her, he appeared to find her amusing.

"I couldn't agree more," he drawled. "Having his parents closely connected would definitely be in Rowdy's best interests."

She pretended not to notice the sexual innuendo. "I'm glad we agree on something." She peered pointedly at the grandfather clock in the corner of the room. "It's late and I have a court hearing early tomorrow, so if there's nothing else you wanted to discuss…?"

"There's a lot I want to discuss with you, but it'll keep." His half smile faded and his expression turned brooding. "Don't ever lie to me again, Jessie."

Guilt assailed her. "I'm sorry, Zach, really. If I could take it back, I would."

"Just don't do it again. And no more making decisions on your own about what I should or shouldn't be told about Rowdy. You're not alone in this."

She nodded, swallowing back tears.

"Good." He cupped her face in his hands, his gaze searching hers. "If you need time to get used to what's between us, Jessie, I'll back off for now. Just don't take too long coming to terms with it. I've waited four years to have you again and it's been four years too long."

He kissed her. Connected only by his hands against her face and his mouth on hers, still Jessie was instantly lost, drowning in the heat that flared to life. Beneath the carnality of the kiss moved a sweetness and longing that took her breath.

At last, he lifted his head. "I'll call you."

He left her, disappearing through the door into the night.

Jessie could only stare after him, tempted and terrified by the promise of pleasure.

Chapter Seven

The following morning in Wolf Creek, Zach finished loading lumber into the bed of his pickup then just before noon, he walked the short three blocks to the Saloon.

"Hi, Zach." Raine Harper greeted him as he entered.

"Raine." He nodded, removing his hat and joining her at the end of the bar. He gestured at the large black book and stack of receipts cradled in her arms. "You must have bookkeeping duty today."

She chuckled. "Yes, a restaurant owner's work is never done. What brings you to town?"

"I picked up a load of lumber for the barn."

"Ah." She smiled. "A rancher's work is never done, either."

"Not when the ranch hasn't been taken care of for years," he replied.

"I'm guessing you can chalk that up to your uncle?"

"That would be my guess," he agreed.

She eyed him, her gaze curious. "Are you going to tell me what brought Chase McCloud in here after you the other day?"

When he didn't answer, Raine shook her head ruefully. "You aren't going to tell me, are you?" When he remained silent, she laughed. "I have to admit, he's the first man I've seen in Wolf Creek that looks tough enough, maybe mean enough, to match you. I'm glad his sister broke things up before the two of you tore up my bar."

"So it's your business you're worried about?" Zach asked easily. "Not my good health?"

"I'm always worried about your good health, Zach." She patted his arm. "It's good to have you back. You were gone too long. See you later." She turned away, waggling her fingers as she disappeared through the door to the stairs that would take her to the office on the building's second floor.

Zach lifted a hand in reply. Although they'd never dated, Raine had been a good friend in high school and was one of the few people, outside his mother and sister, who had welcomed him home.

Seated at a booth near the back of the restaurant, Zach finished a hamburger and fries and was about to drink the last of his coffee when someone halted next to the booth.

"Hello, Zach." Harlan Kerrigan tossed his Stetson onto the bench seat of the booth and followed it, taking a seat across from Zach.

Zach eyed his uncle over the rim of his coffee cup and drank, swallowing before lowering the mug to the tabletop. "Harlan." His tone was neither welcoming nor encouraging.

Harlan wore a Western-tailored brown suit over a crisp white shirt; a bolo tie chased in heavy silver conveyed just the right casual touch of affluence. Zach suspected the clothes were part of his uncle's calculated effort to project an image of a powerful rancher concerned about and connected with the local community.

"I hear you're living out on Section Ten." Harlan caught the eye of the busy waitress, gesturing. "Coffee," he told her when she neared. He waited until she'd filled a mug and set it on the table in front of him before he turned back to Zach. "I suppose you're doing a lot of repair work on the buildings?"

"Some." Zach knew his uncle hadn't sought him out to talk about the condition of his ranch buildings.

"I told Rachel the place was falling down." Harlan shook his head with concern. "I don't know why Dad let the property go so far downhill."

Zach lifted an eyebrow. "So Granddad was responsible for the deteriorated state of Section Ten? That's interesting news. I thought you were the one who made decisions and allocated maintenance funds over the last few years?"

"I ran the company after Dad became ill," Harlan agreed. "But by the time I took over, Kerrigan holdings were in such dire financial difficulties there wasn't enough money to keep all the properties in peak condition." He shrugged. "Section Ten has decent land but none of the family lived there. Naturally, it was a low priority on the maintenance list."

"I see." Zach's response was noncommittal. He knew Harlan would eventually get around to his reason for seeking him out, but he didn't have the patience to wait. He glanced at his watch. "Why don't you tell me why you're really here."

Harlan's eyes narrowed, the affable facade fading to expose hard impatience. "I understand you had a confrontation with Chase McCloud in the Saloon and his sister had to stop a fight."

"I wouldn't call it a confrontation. Exactly."

"Call it whatever you like." Harlan gestured impatiently. "I don't care if you beat the hell out of any of the McClouds. But the gossips say Jessie told her brother something was her fault, and not yours."

Zach didn't answer him, merely waited.

"What connection is there between you and the McCloud girl?"

"That's my business."

The last vestige of pleasantness fell away. Harlan's eyes were cold, his voice icy. "There *is* no business for a Kerrigan with a McCloud."

"Is that right?" Zach felt his muscles tightening.

"I'm the head of this family, now that Dad is gone. Your sister didn't listen to me when she married Luke McCloud but you're a man, not a brainless female. You're smart enough to recognize any connection to a McCloud can only lead to trouble."

"And why is that?"

"Because they've interfered and stood in the way of our family too many times over the years to ever be viewed as anything but the enemy."

"Don't you think it might be time to consider laying down our weapons and calling an end to the feud? Rachel's married to Luke—the families are related, whether you like it or not."

Harlan snorted in contempt. "Rachel will soon find out she can't trust a McCloud. I hope she learns her lesson before she's saddled with a kid. God knows we don't want any McCloud blood mixed with ours."

Zach's temper began to win out over his control. Much as he wanted to keep Harlan talking in hopes he'd reveal his agenda, he wasn't sure how much longer he could listen to his uncle's paranoid ranting. "And why would that be so bad?"

"Use your head, Zach. How many times did

you hear your grandfather say there was room for only one powerful family in this county? He meant for Kerrigans to be that family. It was his dream, and now it's mine. I already influence local politicians and I've laid groundwork at the state level. If we play our cards right, a Kerrigan can be governor of this state." Harlan's eyes gleamed. "Think of it—the Governor's mansion. We could own this state, boy, we could own it!"

"A Kerrigan as governor?" Zach eyed him. "Which Kerrigan—you or Lonnie?"

"Lonnie hasn't the temperament for politics."

"So you're the one who wants to be governor." Zach wondered how much of Harlan's heightened hatred of the McClouds was due to his political aspirations. And why his uncle had decided the McClouds were a threat to his plan to occupy the governor's mansion in Helena.

"It's time this family expanded our influence beyond the surrounding counties. State government is the next natural step."

"If you say so." Zach slid out of the booth, shoving a hand into his jeans pocket to draw out a money clip.

"You didn't tell me what the McCloud girl meant

when she told her brother it wasn't your fault," Harlan reminded him, leaving the booth to stand.

"No, I didn't." Zach's voice lowered, going cold. "And I won't. It's none of your business. You should know if you or Lonnie approaches Jessie about this, I'll take it personally. I want her left alone."

"So there *is* something going on between you and Jessie McCloud." Harlan's ruddy face darkened further as he swore. "Not a smart move, Zach."

"Don't threaten me, Harlan. And stay away from Jessie. You won't like the repercussions if you don't."

Zach threw some bills on the table and left the restaurant before he gave in to temptation and asked Harlan to step into the alley. The urge to underline with his fists his demand that his uncle and cousin leave Jessie alone was compelling but he knew any altercation would only add fuel to the local speculation. Jessie wouldn't like it if he added to the gossip already circulating about them.

At 7:00 a.m., Jessie could hear the phone ringing inside her office while she fumbled with the lock, juggling files, briefcase and purse. She let the door slam shut behind her and dropped her armload atop Tina's desk to grab the receiver.

"McCloud Law Office."

"Hey, Jessie."

"Luke, you're back!"

"We got home last night," Luke confirmed. "I had breakfast with Mom and Dad this morning. You have anything you want to tell me?"

Damn. Her parents must have told him about Zach. "As a matter of fact, I need to talk to both you and Rachel." A thought occurred to her. "Or was Rachel at breakfast, too?"

"No. She slept in this morning. I thought I'd call you before I wake her and tell her she has a nephew. I'm guessing the first thing she'll do is phone her mother and tell her about Rowdy, so you and Zach might want to get your stories straight. I'd expect Rachel and Judith will show up on your doorstep tonight."

"Thanks for the warning. I owe you, Luke."

"Yeah, you do. If I hadn't already crossed the line and married a Kerrigan, I'd be asking you whether you'd lost your mind."

"You can still ask, but I'm not sure I have an answer," she said wryly.

"Dad said Chase went looking for Zach."

"Yes, and he found him in The Saloon. I don't know who was more surprised to see him there, Raine Harper or Zach."

"Raine was there, too?"

"Chase walked out as she walked in. I don't think she was expecting to see a McCloud in her bar, and definitely not two of us at once. She looked a little shell-shocked."

"Yeah, Dad mentioned you were there. I haven't talked to Chase yet. How did he take the news about you and Zach?"

"Not well," Jessie admitted with a sigh. "Not well at all."

"Maybe he'll come around when he's had time to get used to the idea. He's okay with Rachel. In fact, I think he likes her."

"But Rachel's a woman. You know what Granddad said about Kerrigan women."

"He liked them."

"Yes, but he didn't like Kerrigan men," Jessie said gloomily. "In fact, he said they couldn't be trusted."

"He may have been right. Only time will tell."

"Luke," Jessie said anxiously. "I'm counting on

you to help me with Chase. You're closer to him than anyone else, plus you know what it's like to break the rules of the feud."

"You're asking a lot, Jessie. In the first place, if Zach wasn't my wife's brother, I'd be looking for him right now, too. I'm not convinced he couldn't have found out about Rowdy earlier. He should have made sure you weren't pregnant. Hell, he should have made sure you didn't *get* pregnant. At the very least, he had an obligation to make sure you were okay."

Jessie blew out a deep breath and rolled her eyes. "You, Chase and Dad must be members of a very, very small club left over from the last century. You do realize that lots of men and women have one-night stands and then part, never seeing each other again?"

"I know some men do. But that doesn't mean I'm going to stand by and let some SOB treat my sister that way." His tone was grim.

Jessie sighed loudly. "I love you guys, I really do. But you've got to get over your compulsion to wrap me in cotton and shield me from the world."

Her heavy sigh and long-suffering tone made Luke laugh.

"All right, all right," he conceded. "I won't punch Zach the next time I see him—that should make both you and Rachel happy. But the jury's still out on whether he'll ever be welcome at Mom's house for Sunday dinner."

"He doesn't need to be. He's not my husband. All I ask of you is to be polite to each other for Rowdy's sake."

"We'll see. I have to go wake up Rachel and break the news. Expect to see her on your front porch sometime today or tonight."

"Thanks for the warning."

Jessie hung up, staring at the phone with unseeing eyes while she tried to envision the unavoidable scene. She hadn't officially met Zach's mother although Rachel spoke of her often. Jessie had assumed from Rachel's comments that theirs was a strong mother-daughter relationship and that Judith was a kind woman with a sense of humor. Nevertheless, she thought, how likely is it that Judith Kerrigan won't be shocked and angry to learn her grandson has been living in the same town without her knowledge? For that matter, how likely was it that *Rachel* wouldn't be angry over the situation?

She gathered up her briefcase, purse and the

files that had slipped and lay scattered over the surface of Tina's desk, and walked into her office. She dropped the collection on her own desktop and picked up the phone.

Listening to the rings, she sat down behind the desk and toed off her comfortable running shoes. Pulling a pair of black heels from her bag, she bent to slip her toes into one.

On the fifth ring, Zach answered with a brusque hello.

"Zach. I'm so glad I caught you before you left the house."

"You almost didn't. I only came in to grab a bandage."

Jessie snapped erect, the remaining sling-back pump forgotten in her hand. "A bandage? What's wrong?"

"Nothing much. I had an argument with Ransom. He won."

"He bit you?" she demanded.

"No, he didn't bite me." Amusement colored his words. "What made you think he might have bitten me?"

"Luke told me Ransom bites people he doesn't like."

"Well, he likes me just fine. He crowded me in his stall and I scraped my shoulder against a post."

"Oh." Jessie frowned at the relief that washed over her. Why should she care if he was hurt or not? She didn't. Did she?

"So what's up?" Zach prompted.

His question snapped her out of her distraction. "Luke just called. My parents told him about you and Rowdy over breakfast this morning."

"So Rachel knows?"

"I'm sure she does by now. He was going to tell her as soon as he hung up. He warned me to expect both Rachel and your mother's arrival on my doorstep tonight."

"Sounds like he knows my mom and sister well," Zach commented, his voice dry.

"I wanted to warn you, too, in case you feel you need to talk to your mother and Rachel before they arrive. Or if you'd like to be there when they meet Rowdy?"

"Are you sure you want them to come to your house? Would you rather have my mother meet Rowdy for the first time on neutral territory?"

"Like where?"

"Like here. There's no reason why we can't arrange for them to come to my place, if you'd be more comfortable."

Jessie thought quickly. "That's a good idea. Then I could take Rowdy and leave if I felt he needed a break. And would you warn them not to say anything to Rowdy about his being family since we haven't told him yet?"

"Jessie." His voice roughened, warmed with reassurance. "Don't spend your day worrying about this. They might be upset but they're not going to say anything in front of Rowdy. In fact, if you'd rather they not ask you any questions, I'll call them both today. Anything they want to know about our situation, they can ask me."

Relief flooded over her. "That would be wonderful, Zach. It's not that I want to dodge their questions forever, but during this initial visit with Rowdy it might be best if we could focus on him."

"I'll tell them. No questions. What time do you want to meet them here?"

Jessie flipped open her calendar. "My last appointment is at two o'clock. I can pick up Rowdy from the Harrises' and be at your place around three or three-thirty. Will that work?"

"Sounds good to me. I'll call Rachel and

Mom." He laughed a deep, rueful chuckle. "Who am I kidding? I won't have to phone them. I'm sure they'll call me."

The bell on the outer office door jingled and Jessie heard Tina enter the reception area, followed by the familiar sounds of her secretary's morning routine.

"I have to go. Will you let me know if we need to change the time?"

Zach assured her he would and she hung up. A headache was beginning to pound at her temples and she slipped her left shoe on and pulled open a desk drawer to take out aspirin.

The day flew by much too quickly. Jessie's last appointment took longer than she'd anticipated and by the time she raced home, collected Rowdy from next door, changed her clothes and coaxed him into a clean shirt and shorts, it was almost three-thirty. She buckled Rowdy into his car seat, then dialed Zach on her cell phone as she drove out of town. The answering machine picked up.

"Hi, Zach, this is Jessie. I'm running late but we're on our way."

Zach was sitting on the shaded porch of his

house with Rachel, Judith and Luke when Jessie drove down the lane and parked just outside the fence.

"Look, Mommy, Aunt Rachel's here—and so is Uncle Luke!" Rowdy said with delight.

"I know, hon. How nice that we'll get to see them." Jessie waved at the quartet as she left the SUV and opened Rowdy's door. He wriggled impatiently while she unbuckled the straps to release him from the car seat.

Zach walked down the steps, reaching the vehicle just as Rowdy jumped out, his scuffed tennis shoes sending gravel scattering.

"Hey, bud." Zach tousled Rowdy's mop of dark hair. "Glad you could come out this afternoon. The puppies have grown a lot since the last time you were here."

"Can we see them?" Rowdy asked eagerly.

"Sure. But first, you and your mom should come say hello to your Aunt Rachel and Uncle Luke." Zach looked at Jessie, his gaze assessing.

She managed to smile despite the butterflies dancing in her stomach. Evidently, her effort to appear calm didn't fool Zach because he settled a protective arm around her middle and turned her gently toward the porch and the three people standing there, waiting. Taking Rowdy's hand in his, he walked between them through the gate and up the walk to the porch. The warmth of his hand against her waist steadied her.

"Hi, Rowdy." Rachel's cheerful greeting carried a faint tremor.

"Hi, Aunt Rachel. Hi, Uncle Luke." Rowdy pulled free of Zach's light hold and ran up the steps. He halted in front of Rachel and Luke, beaming up at them. "Where's Uncle Chase?"

"He's working with Grandpa John today, branding cattle."

"Oh. Uncle Zach and me are gonna go see the puppies. You can come with us if you want."

"I'd love to." Rachel smiled down at him.

Zach and Jessie joined them on the porch and he gave Jessie's waist a quick, reassuring squeeze. "Mom, I don't think you've met Jessie. Jessie, this is my mother, Judith."

"Hello, Mrs. Kerrigan." Jessie felt measured and assessed as the petite, older woman stared at her. Then Judith smiled. Faint and reserved though it was, nevertheless, it held no hostility. Jessie felt a weight lift from her shoulders.

"It's nice to meet you, Jessie." Judith held out her hand. "Rachel has told me a lot about you."

Their handshake was brief. "She's mentioned you often, as well, Mrs. Kerrigan."

"And this is Rowdy, Mom," Zach interrupted. He cupped his hands over the little boy's small shoulders and turned him toward Judith. "This is my mother. Her name is Judith."

"Hello, there," Judith Kerrigan said softly. Her voice wasn't entirely steady.

"Hi." Rowdy stared up at her. "Do you like puppies?"

"Yes, I do, very much."

"You can come see the puppies with us. But we have to be quiet so we don't scare the mommy and we can't hold them unless Uncle Zach says it's okay." He twisted to look up at his father. "Can she hold a puppy?"

"Sure."

"Okay." Rowdy nodded, the matter clearly settled in his opinion. "Can we go now?"

Zach nodded gravely. "I think now would be good. Are you coming with us, Jessie? Rachel?"

Jessie glanced at her silent brother. His face was impassive. She met Rachel's gaze and read the turmoil in her sister-in-law's eyes. "Why don't you three go ahead, Zach. I'll stay here with Rachel and Luke for a few minutes."

Zach hesitated, looking from his sister to Jessie. "Are you sure?"

She nodded. "I'm sure. We'll be along in a few minutes to visit the puppies with you, Rowdy."

Luke leaned against the porch post and Rachel stood next to Jessie. All three were silent, their eyes trained on Rowdy as he skipped down the sidewalk ahead of Zach and Judith.

"How could you have kept him from us?" Rachel said softly, careful lest her voice carry to the trio making their way across the dusty ranch yard toward the barn.

"I didn't feel I had a choice. Until you married Luke, I was convinced keeping silent was the right thing—the only thing—to do," Jessie said. Zach slid open the big door and followed Rowdy and Judith inside the barn, ending any possibility of their conversation being overheard. "There's a legacy of hate between our families—I couldn't see any way for the McClouds and the Kerrigans to share a grandchild. I studied domestic case law—I know what a nightmare a child's life can become when families hate each other. Given the history between ours, it seemed an impossible situation."

"But you didn't even let Zach know he was a father. And my mother… If you only knew how much she's looked forward to having grandchildren." Rachel's eyes were dark with pain and accusation.

"I couldn't have told your mother and you without Harlan and Lonnie finding out. I'm more sorry than I can say that you've been hurt, Rachel, but if I had it to do all over again…well, I don't know. Maybe I would have told Zach. Maybe he would have come home. Maybe he would have kept Harlan and Lonnie in line." Jessie lifted her hands helplessly, then let them fall to her side once again. "But maybe it wouldn't have worked out that way."

"Zach and Luke would never have allowed my uncle or cousin to harm you or Rowdy!" Rachel protested.

"You thought *I* wouldn't have protected you from Lonnie?" Luke's voice was incredulous, laced with anger.

"I'm sure you would have protected us, as

would Chase and Dad," Jessie agreed. "But at what cost? You know Lonnie. What's the likelihood he wouldn't have taken every opportunity to tell people that Rowdy's illegitimate? Or have used worse language about both Rowdy and me? And if he had, you guys would have gone ballistic." Jessie sighed, combing her hair off her temples with her fingers. "How many times would one of you have gone to jail for assaulting Lonnie, or maybe even Harlan? In another two years, Rowdy will start school. I don't want him struggling with fallout from the feud that nearly destroyed our family once before. And I never, under any circumstances, want to watch a brother of mine be taken to jail again."

Luke and Rachel were silent.

"You know I'm right," Jessie said at last. "Your marriage created a truce between our family and you, Rachel. That acceptance includes your mother, but not Harlan and Lonnie. And there's no guarantee it will extend to Zach."

"Of course it will," Rachel said promptly. "He's nothing like my uncle and cousin. And he's tied to your family through Rowdy, just as I'm tied to the McClouds through my marriage to Luke."

Luke and Jessie exchanged a swift significant look.

Rachel noticed and frowned. "What?" she demanded. "Don't you agree Zach is outside the feud, just like Mom and me?"

Luke slung his arm around her shoulders and pressed a kiss to her temple. "You're a woman, Rachel."

"What does that have to do with anything?" Bewildered, she met Jessie's gaze. When Jessie remained silent, Rachel turned to Luke. "Tell me."

"At least two people lied about what happened the night Mike Harper died. Those two were Harlan and Lonnie. But we've always thought Marcus knew, too. That makes three out of four Kerrigan men who were directly responsible for Chase spending time in jail."

"But Zach didn't have anything to do with any of that," Rachel protested. "He was only fifteen when Mike was killed and he and Lonnie hated each other. Besides, Zach was rarely home during those years we lived at my grandfather's house— he spent most of his time working with Charlie Ankrum in the barns, and so did I."

"Nevertheless, because of your uncle and

cousin, Chase paid a terrible price for a crime he didn't commit. He's not likely to trust anyone named Kerrigan."

"Are you saying he doesn't like me? That he's faking when he comes to visit?" Rachel looked horrified.

"No! No, honey, Chase doesn't fake anything. If he didn't genuinely like you, you'd know it."

"You're an exception, Rachel," Jessie tried to explain. "But it's not likely Chase will ever accept Zach the way he has you. And because of that, I still don't know how I'm going to make the situation with Zach, Rowdy and myself work. I'm sure we will," she hastened to add when Rachel's face fell. "I just don't know how we can do it with any degree of comfort."

"I don't know, either," Luke said. "But there's no quick fix and nothing we can do, Rachel, so please don't worry."

Rachel smiled ruefully. "Me? Not worry? You've got to be kidding."

Luke chuckled. "Why don't we join your mom and Rowdy in the barn."

He slipped his hand into Rachel's, waved Jessie ahead of them, and the three left the house to find the puppies and Rowdy.

Jessie drove home two hours later. Rowdy seemed to be catching a summer cold and drooped in his car seat, sniffing and complaining from the backseat. Rowdy meeting his grandmother for the first time had seemed to go well, she thought. If only everything else about this situation could follow suit.

Zach had a series of emergencies over the next two days. Cattle broke out of the North Pasture, drifting down the county road before he knew they'd escaped. He and Charlie spent a long, frustrating day rounding them up and herding them to safety before replacing half a dozen fence posts. It was long after dark on the second day by the time he finished stringing new wire and catching up on the work that had been put on hold. Having returned to the house just after 10:00 p.m., he stacked ham and cheese between thick slices of his mother's homemade bread and carried it upstairs with him. A half hour later, he pulled on clean jeans over cotton briefs and walked downstairs, rubbing a towel over his still-damp hair.

Was it too late to call Jessie? The urge to check on her, to find out if she'd been reassured by meeting his mother or if she was still worried, had nagged him since her SUV had disappeared down the highway two days earlier.

He looked at the wall clock above the bookcase. The hands pointed to 10:35 p.m.

"What the hell," he muttered. He slung the damp towel over his bare shoulder and picked up the phone. If she was sleeping, he'd apologize and hang up. If she was awake...

"Hello?"

"Jessie?" Zach heard a child crying fretfully in the background. "Is that Rowdy?"

"Yes. I can't talk right now, Zach. We're on our way out the door." She sounded hurried, worried and exhausted.

"What's wrong?" Zach demanded.

"Rowdy's running a fever—his temperature is 103. I've tried everything and can't get it down. I'm taking him to the emergency room at Wolf Creek General."

"I'll meet you there. Are you sure you're okay to drive?"

"Of course I can drive—you don't have to

come to the hospital, Zach, I'm sure Rowdy will be fine—"

"I'll be there," he interrupted her. "Drive carefully."

He hung up and raced upstairs. He yanked a T-shirt over his head and pulled on socks and boots before grabbing his wallet and truck keys from the dressertop. He snatched a long-sleeved shirt from a hanger in the closet and shrugged into it on his way down the stairs, closing the snaps up the front as he left the porch and jogged to his truck.

He broke speed limits on his way into town and reached the nearly empty parking lot of the hospital in record time. Jessie's SUV was parked just outside the emergency room door. He slotted his truck into the space next to it and strode quickly through the double doors. The waiting room was empty and silent. There was no sign of Jessie and no nurse sat behind the counter.

Zach had had his share of childhood visits to this room for broken bones. He didn't stop to ring the bell at the nurse's counter. Instead, he strode through another set of double doors into the treatment room beyond. The hospital was small but well equipped and the emergency area held six stations. All but one had curtains drawn back to reveal empty gurneys. At the far end of the room a doctor, nurse and Jessie stood around a bed. The slight, still figure beneath the blanket was surely Rowdy and Zach's heart clenched with sheer terror. He wasn't…?

His boots thumped against the tiled floor. Jessie looked over her shoulder.

"Zach!" Relief erased worry from her pale features.

She didn't protest when he reached her and wrapped his arms around her, holding her tight. The band around his chest eased as he realized Rowdy was asleep, his round cheeks flushed with fever, his breathing faint rasps of sound in the quiet room.

"How is he?"

"His cold progressed to ear infections, in both ears." Jessie sounded exhausted. "No wonder he hasn't been able to sleep."

"The cough medicine I prescribed will ease the coughing and allow him to rest," the doctor put in. "And the antibiotics we've started him on will take care of the infection. I can admit him and we can keep him here in the hospital overnight for observation, or you can take him home. It's your decision." The doctor paused, his keen gaze assessing Jessie. "He's liable to be wakeful during the night until the antibiotic has a chance to work. That means someone will be getting up with him, and you look as tired as Rowdy. You might want to let him stay in hospital, and get some rest yourself."

"I'll stay with them."

Jessie had been leaning heavily against Zach, giving him the impression she was nearly asleep on her feet, so tired and possibly grateful for his support that she'd forgotten he bore her weight. At his words, she stiffened, easing away to arm's length although she swayed with the effort.

"You don't need to, Zach, I—"

"I know you could do this on your own if you had to," he interrupted. "The point is, you don't have to. I'll be glad to help." He held her gaze with his. "I *want* to help, Jessie."

She nodded slowly.

"Excellent," the doctor said briskly. "In that case, Rowdy can recuperate at home." He tucked three plastic medicine vials into a bag and handed it to Jessie. "Call me if you have any questions or if his fever starts to rise again. Otherwise, I'll see him in my office for a checkup in two days."

He was interrupted by loud voices in the outer room.

"Where the hell is the doctor?"

Someone pounded repeatedly on the bell at the desk. A crash was followed by raucous laughter and accompanied by a string of curse words.

"Sounds like we've got another emergency. Good luck, you two." He nodded at the nurse and she preceded him out of the room.

"I'll carry Rowdy out to your car," Zach said quietly.

Jessie agreed and turned to pick up her purse and light sweater from the chair by the bed. Zach pulled back the hospital sheet and bent to slip his arms under Rowdy, picking him up. The little boy murmured in protest but didn't wake, laying his head trustingly on Zach's shoulder and going back to sleep. His little body felt boneless, his arm limp where it circled Zach's neck. For one brief moment, Zach was swamped with emotion. This was his son.

He looked at Jessie and felt the same fierce, possessive surge. *Mine.* The urge to claim and keep swept away the remnants of his anger at Jessie. He'd missed three years of Rowdy's life. He refused to waste any more time without him. Without *them*.

She thought he wanted only Rowdy in his life. She was wrong.

Zach shouldered open the door to the outer waiting room, holding it for Jessie to walk through.

"Well, well." Lonnie Kerrigan stood at the reception desk, swaying on his feet while blood dripped onto the tile floor from a gash in his arm. He leered at Jessie. "What are you doing with my cousin? And who's the kid?"

"None of your business, Lonnie," Zach said curtly, stepping between him and Jessie.

"Here's your insurance card, Mr. Kerrigan," the nurse interjected. She bustled around the desk and took his injured arm. "You're bleeding all over my clean floor." She wrapped a white towel around Lonnie's forearm. The doctor joined her and took his other arm, turning him forcefully toward the inner door.

"Hey, don't push me," he objected, gesturing at Zach and Jessie. "This is my cousin. Do you know my cousin? I don't know who the kid is, but the three of them look like a cozy little family, don't they?"

The nurse grimaced and leaned away from him. The doctor caught him when he staggered and lurched sideways. "You're drunk, Mr. Kerrigan. I suggest we get your arm stitched up before you fall down and do more damage to your body."

Despite Lonnie's lack of cooperation, they walked him to the doors leading to the patient care area. Lonnie continued to ogle Jessie over his shoulder with blatant sexual appraisal. "Too bad you're a McCloud, honey. We could have fun, you and me."

Zach held on to his temper by a thread. He didn't want to upset Jessie or Rowdy any further after the night they'd had, but he badly wanted to stop Lonnie's mouth with his fist.

"Lonnie Kerrigan is a pig."

Jessie's calm, matter-of-fact statement carried no heat and was spoken with such conviction that Zach laughed out loud.

"You're right. Although calling him a pig is probably an insult to pigs everywhere. Let's get out of here."

Minutes later, Zach had Rowdy tucked into his

car seat, his beloved, tattered blanket draped over him while he clutched one corner, his eyes closed, asleep.

Zach shut the door on Rowdy with a quiet thunk.

"I'll drive," he told Jessie. "You're nearly asleep on your feet."

"What about your truck?"

"I'll pick it up in the morning." He took the SUV keys from her unresisting fingers, pulled open the front passenger door, and urged her inside. It was a testament to how difficult the last few nights with Rowdy must have been when she didn't protest.

"Thank you for being here, Zach," she said drowsily. "Even though I told you not to come."

He glanced at her. Her head tilted sideways against the headrest and she was instantly asleep. Independent and difficult to the end, he thought wryly.

Chapter Eight

"We're home, Jessie." When she didn't respond, Zach gently shook her shoulder. "Wake up, Jess."

She stirred, her lashes lifting to reveal drowsy, heavy-lidded eyes.

"I'll carry Rowdy. Can you make it inside on your own?"

"Yes." She blinked, her eyes more focused and aware, and unlatched her seat belt.

Zach managed to extricate Rowdy from his car

seat without waking him and carried his slight weight, following Jessie up the sidewalk and across the porch. Inside, the house was quiet and dark, with only one lamp lit. The small pool of pale gold light in the corner threw shadows over the rest of the living room and lightened the dimness of the hallway beyond.

Jessie led the way down the hall to Rowdy's bedroom where a night-light glowed softly, barely illuminating the white-painted dresser and toy chest. She turned down the sheet on the narrow child's bed and Zach carefully eased Rowdy from his shoulder and onto the mattress. The little boy murmured incoherently and curled against the pillow, still clutching the bunched-up corner of his blanket in one fist. Since he'd worn his pajamas to the hospital and his feet were bare, there was no need to strip daytime clothing from him; Zach pulled the sheet up and tucked it around his waist. Jessie bent and kissed his cheek, her eyes closing briefly before she stood erect and walked to the door, where she leaned wearily against the jamb.

Zach brushed a shock of dark hair from Rowdy's forehead and leaned over the bed, breathing in the little-boy smell of clean pajamas, soap and cherry-flavored medicine. He brushed his lips against the downy cheek, frowning at the heat beneath the soft skin before he joined Jessie.

"He still feels warm," he whispered, turning to look back at the bed and its tiny occupant.

"I know. He's not nearly as hot as he was but he's still running a fever," she said softly, covering a yawn with her hand.

"You need to sleep." Zach took her by the shoulders and gently turned her into the hall, pulling Rowdy's door nearly closed. "Which way to your bedroom?"

She hesitated, worry and indecision flitting across her features. Before she could speak, Zach brushed the tip of his forefinger over her lips, silencing her. "I'm going to take you to your room and make sure you go to bed. That's all. In fact, why don't you tell me where I can find an extra pillow and a blanket before I tuck you in. I'll crash on your sofa tonight."

He thought he glimpsed a fleeting hint of regret in the relief that eased her expression and drained the tension from her shoulders. Then she stepped away from him and opened a closet across the hall.

"Here's a pillow," she whispered. He took it from her and she stacked a light blanket on top before closing the door carefully so as not to wake Rowdy. "My bedroom is the next room down."

Zach followed her, stopping in the doorway while Jessie moved around the bed and switched on a lamp. The bedroom was feminine and seductive, the woman standing in the small spill of light by the bed even more so. She looked at him, hesitating, her blue eyes shadowed.

He'd never wanted a woman this badly. It was all he could do to stay put and not go to her. But she was exhausted and vulnerable and he couldn't take advantage of her, no matter how tempted he was.

"Get your pajamas on." His voice was gravelly, much lower than its normal deep tone. "I'll leave as soon as you're in bed."

She looked skeptical but pulled open a dresser drawer and took out a pink top and pants. She moved past him in the doorway, careful not to touch him, and disappeared into the adjoining bathroom.

He waited, listening to the gentle sounds of water running, drawers quietly opening and closing, before the door opened and she walked by him once again.

Zach didn't step aside and although the doorway was wide enough to allow her passage without brushing against him, he was able to inhale her scent and feel the warmth of silky hair against his biceps. Then she was past him, crossing the room and climbing into the bed.

Wondering briefly just how much torture he could take, he followed her and switched off the lamp. "Go to sleep. Don't worry about Rowdy. If he wakes up, I'll handle it, and I'll give him the medicine on schedule."

"Thank you, Zach."

Her quiet words reached him at the door and he paused to look back. "You're welcome. Good night."

He stepped into the hall and closed the door behind him. For several long moments, he just stood there, willing himself not to go back inside and climb in bed with her. Finally, he moved silently toward the living room, pausing to check on the still-sleeping Rowdy.

He tossed the pillow on the end of the sofa and sat down to pull off his boots before he stretched out, tugging the blanket over his legs and up to his waist. The house was quiet, without a sound to break the stillness. Zach felt an odd contentment and sense of rightness that his son and Jessie slept down the hall while he kept watch.

Sunshine poured through the window, slanting across the bed. Jessie woke and sat upright, puzzled at the unaccustomed sunlight in her bedroom. Why had she left the blinds open last night?

Rowdy! She leaped out of bed and ran down the hall to his room but the bed was empty, the sheets rumpled. She found him on the sofa in the living room, sprawled on top of Zach. Both of them were sound asleep, Zach's arms loosely holding Rowdy safely against his chest, one big hand splayed over his back.

She propped herself against the doorjamb, her eyes misting.

I'm in love with him, she thought with sudden, painful insight. *I've loved him since the night Rowdy was conceived. And he's going to break my heart.*

She remained in the doorway for long moments, watching the two sleep, before she could pull herself away. Zach had been a rock of support last night and she couldn't help but wish they were a normal couple, raising a child they both loved, sharing their lives. This wasn't Rowdy's first illness but it was the first time she hadn't dealt with it alone.

How could she mourn the loss of something she'd never had, she wondered. Yet, she did. If she'd contacted Zach when she learned she was pregnant, if she hadn't lied, maybe they would have married and become a family.

Or maybe not.

Jessie stood in the shower, the hot water pouring over her, easing tense muscles. The likelihood there could ever be a future for her with Zach was a million to one. Her family would never approve of him as her husband—they weren't doing very well coping with the fact that he was Rowdy's father. But even if a miracle occurred and her family, especially Chase, accepted Zach, she couldn't believe Zach would be willing to forgive and forget. She'd lied to him. He might want to sleep with her but that didn't mean he'd ever love and trust her.

She turned off the water and toweled off, dressing in a pale-green tank top paired with a patterned green cotton skirt, the bare top and flirty short skirt cool in the morning heat. She applied mascara and lipgloss before she left the bathroom and moved quietly on bare feet into the kitchen. Chase and Rowdy slept on in the living room while she started breakfast.

"Good morning." The deep voice was gravelly with sleep.

Jessie looked over her shoulder. Zach stood just inside the kitchen door, his dark hair messy, eyes sleepy and stubble shadowing his jaw, holding Rowdy's hand.

"Hi, Mommy."

"Hey." Jessie smiled at the big, dangerous-looking man and the small, grinning little boy, and turned down the heat under the skillet where sausage sizzled and spat as it cooked. "You woke up just in time. Breakfast is almost ready."

She held out her arms and Rowdy ran across the kitchen. She caught him and picked him up, giving him a hug before settling him on her hip. "How are you feeling?"

"Good." He nodded firmly before coughing.

"Is it time for medicine?" Jessie asked Zach.

He glanced at the clock on the wall. "Not for another hour."

Rowdy coughed again. "Cover your mouth, sweetie," Jessie said. Rowdy immediately clapped his hand over his mouth, then took it away to cough once more. Jessie cupped her palm over his lips and nose and he grimaced.

Zach watched the interplay, a lazy smile on his face.

"Do I have time for a quick shower?" he asked.

"Absolutely. Clean towels are in the hall linen closet."

"Thanks—I won't be long."

Jessie settled Rowdy at the table with a sippy cup of milk and half a breakfast bar, waiting until she heard the shower turn off before pouring scrambled eggs into a hot skillet. By the time Zach returned to the kitchen, breakfast was on the table.

"Perfect timing." She carried the thermal coffeepot to the table, slipping into her customary seat. "Rowdy wants you to sit by him."

"Is that right?" Zach ruffled Rowdy's hair and took the chair next to him and across from Jessie.

Breakfast was a quiet affair. Rowdy still had a slight fever and his usual chattiness was subdued but he drank his orange juice and managed to finish several bites of eggs and toast. When he yawned, Jessie gave him a teaspoonful of cherry-flavored medicine and carried him down the hall to tuck him into bed again.

Zach was clearing the table when she returned to the kitchen.

"Is he asleep?" he asked, gathering the plates and cutlery.

"Not yet, but he will be before long." Jessie ran water in the sink and began to rinse dishes. "He could barely keep his eyes open." She glanced up when he set the stack of plates on the counter next to her. "Did he wake up often during the night?"

"No more than four or five times." Zach shrugged. "Not bad considering how much he was coughing. I got up with him for the last time around four this morning and he didn't want to go back to bed so I let him sleep with me on the sofa."

"And you actually slept?" Jessie lifted an eyebrow in disbelief. "I'm impressed. He's been known to push me right out of bed and onto the floor."

Zach grinned. "It was a little dicey at first but I finally talked him into lying on my chest and he settled down—one minute he was awake and the next, he was dead asleep."

"I didn't hear either of you during the night. I was so tired, I don't think I would have been able to wake up if he'd needed me. Thanks for staying and taking care of him, Zach."

"My pleasure." He took the last of the rinsed plates from her hands and slotted them into the dishwasher before closing the door. He leaned his hip against the counter, crossed his arms over his chest and eyed her, his face set in stern lines. "We need to talk, Jessie."

Her heart stuttered. "About Rowdy? What's wrong?"

"Nothing—it's not about Rowdy. At least, not directly, although he's involved."

"Then—what?"

"I think we should get married."

Jessie felt her mouth drop open, her eyes widen as she stared at him. "What?" she managed to get out.

"You heard me." Zach's gaze held hers. "Think how much better it would be for Rowdy if there were two of us to look after him. You were exhausted last night, so tired you were staggering. If I'd known he was ill, I would have been here earlier and we could have taken turns caring for him."

"I don't know what to say, Zach." She bit her lip, knocked off balance by his proposal. "Did you decide this just last night?"

"The trip to the E.R. last night convinced me, but the time I've spent with you and Rowdy over the last weeks has made me realize how much work it is to take care of him. I don't want to be a part-time father, Jessie. I want to be there when he's tucked into bed at night and have breakfast with him every morning. I want to be part of his life every day."

"I'm not sure it would work," Jessie began, painfully aware of the irony that Zach had decided marriage was a rational step for them on the very morning she realized she loved him.

"Why not?"

"Because children need a calm, loving atmosphere in their home and you hate me, Zach," she said bluntly.

He looked shocked. "I don't hate you. What in God's name makes you think I hate you?"

"Maybe *hate* is too strong a word, but you're certainly harboring resentment toward me for not telling you about Rowdy."

"I'll get over it."

"I doubt it." She swept her hair back from her forehead in agitation. "And frankly, I'm not sure I want to spend the rest of my life with a man who's trying to get past seriously disliking me."

"I don't seriously dislike you," he growled, clearly annoyed.

"You'll have to forgive me if I find your answer less than convincing."

He eyed her for a moment, then moved so quickly she didn't have time to evade him. He pinned her against the counter, his arms bracketing her to keep her from escaping. "I don't hate you. I don't seriously dislike you." His face was inches from hers as he spoke each word clearly and precisely. "You drive me crazy and half the time you're so damned stubborn I want to throttle you. That does *not* mean I hate you. I don't like it that you lied to me and if you ever do it again, I guarantee we'll have one helluva fight. That does *not* mean I dislike you." He paused, pinning her gaze with his. "Are you getting any of this?"

"Yes."

"Good." His lashes lowered, half masking his eyes. "There's another reason you should marry me, Jessie."

He crowded her against the counter, the worn fabric of his jeans softly abrasive against her bare legs, his hips settling against the cove of hers. The tips of her breasts brushed his chest, nipples hardening painfully, and she was having trouble breathing. "What's that?" she murmured.

"This." With slow precision, he fitted his mouth to hers.

Jessie stopped breathing entirely, totally focused on the slow, seductive wooing of his lips over hers. She slipped her arms around his neck to hold him closer. His hair was cool and silky beneath her fingers. Zach caught her waist and picked her up, sitting her on the countertop without breaking the kiss. Then he nudged her knees apart and stepped between them, pulling her closer until she was flush against his body. Jessie wrapped her legs around his waist and he went still, his grip on her thigh tightening.

"Jessie." His voice was thick. "Take me to bed."

She could no more deny him now than on that

long-ago night in Missoula. "Yes." She barely breathed the word.

He lifted her off the countertop and carried her down the hall. With every step he took, the sensitive vee of her thighs rubbed against the hard proof of his arousal. He reached her bedroom and nudged the door half-closed, then stopped.

"What about Rowdy?"

"He'll sleep for at least an hour, probably two."

"Good." He used his elbow to push the door closed before he walked to the bed and lowered her onto the mattress. Her legs were still wrapped around his waist and she was reluctant to release him. She pulled at his T-shirt, slipping her hands beneath to stroke the sleek, hard muscles. He caught her tank top and tugged it over her head before his mouth closed heatedly over the silk and lace bra covering her breast.

Jessie moaned, arching beneath him. Zach released the front hook and peeled the bra away, tossing it over his shoulder. He sat back on his heels, breathing heavily while he traced the curve of her bare breast with his fingers.

"You are so damned beautiful."

Jessie barely registered the words, so caught up was she in the movement of his hand. Where he touched, she burned.

He pushed up her skirt and slid her panties down her legs, bending to press his mouth against the soft inner skin of her thigh above her knee. The skirt quickly followed the panties. She moaned and reached for him.

He lifted away from her, his eyes hot and intent on her bare body as he peeled off his T-shirt and threw it on the floor, then unzipped his jeans. He shifted off the bed long enough to slide jeans and underwear down his legs, pausing to take a foil packet from his pocket and remove the contents. Then he was back, his warm weight pressing her into the bed, his hair-roughened thighs wedging hers apart once more.

She tensed as he entered her, her hands clenching his biceps.

He brushed soft kisses over her face, soothing her, and his hand slipped between them, stroking her until her muscles loosened and she lifted against him.

"Please," she murmured, pulling his mouth back to hers.

Jessie was incapable of thinking. She screamed and would have woken Rowdy if Zach hadn't covered her mouth and swallowed the sound.

They made love twice, leaving the bedroom to shower and dress before Rowdy woke again.

"I forgot to turn on the dishwasher," Jessie commented, pushing the select buttons.

"We were busy." Zach slipped his arms around her waist and pulled her back against him while his mouth explored the sensitive skin below her ear.

"We were, weren't we." She closed her eyes, trying to breathe. Her eyes opened wide and she twisted in his arms to look up at him. "Oh, my God. What about Rowdy?"

"What about him?" Zach cocked his head, listening. "Not a sound. He's still asleep."

"I know, but what if he'd wakened and come into the bedroom while we…" Her voice trailed off and she flushed under his lazy grin.

"While we were in bed? Honey, parents must deal with that possibility all the time. Otherwise, I doubt there'd ever be more than one kid in a family."

"You don't think we were irresponsible?"

"No, I don't." He cupped the back of her head in his hand and kissed her, his mouth seducing hers. When he lifted his head, she was breathless. "And I plan to be irresponsible as often as possible, so get used to it."

"Get used to it?" She quirked an eyebrow and pushed away from him. "Does that approach usually work with women?"

He laughed. "I don't know but I thought it was worth a try." He sobered, crossing his arms and leaning against the counter. "I want to tell Rowdy today, Jessie. I think it's time."

She stared at him, torn. "What will we do if he doesn't take it well?"

"We'll deal with that if it happens, but I don't think it will. He likes me, Jess."

She bit her lip. "You're right, he does," she conceded slowly. Was she making too much of this? Rowdy had taken to Zach as if he'd known him forever. Was she hesitating because she was afraid for Rowdy, or because she wasn't sure how she'd deal with Zach publicly claiming Rowdy? "All right. We'll tell him after his nap."

Zach's eyes lit with relief and he wrapped his arms around her in a fierce hug. He clearly had no worries about Rowdy's reaction. Jessie wasn't so sure.

The monitor sitting on the kitchen countertop, connected to Rowdy's bedroom, made rustling sounds, then Rowdy's voice came clearly over the small speaker.

"Mommy!"

The moment of truth had arrived sooner than Jessie had expected. "Well…" She pushed out of Zach's arms. "Let's go get him."

Zach followed her, stopping in the doorway while Jessie picked up the sleepy-eyed little boy. She carried him back into the living room and sat on the sofa with Rowdy tucked on her lap. Zach sat beside her, his arm on the sofa behind her, half-turned to face them. Rowdy eyed him but didn't object, though he burrowed deeper into Jessie's arms, still not fully awake.

He wasn't a child who bounced out of bed chipper and fully aware. Jessie chatted with Zach, asking him innocuous questions about the weather and the status of repairs on his ranch buildings until Rowdy stirred against her and sat up.

"I'm hungry," he announced.

She looked at him, smiling when he dropped his blanket on the sofa and eyed her expectantly.

"We'll get a snack in a minute, but first, Zach and I have something to tell you."

"Okay." He looked at Zach, his eyes wide and trusting, his expression curious.

"Remember when we talked about how your daddy worked far away across the ocean?"

"Uh-huh. And you said he had a very 'portant job and he couldn't come home right away."

"That's right." Jessie looked up at Zach. "How would you like it if I told you he's home now and he'd like very much to spend time with you."

Rowdy's instant smile slowly gave way to a frown. "That's okay, I guess, but Uncle Zach and me have to check on the puppies because I've been sick and haven't seen them for a long time."

"That's right," Zach said gravely when Jessie's eyes misted, her smile trembling at Rowdy's matter-of-fact comment. "It's been several days since you checked in on Zarina and we probably have other important guy things to do, too."

Reassured by Rowdy's response, Jessie decided to be blunt. "We've been saving this as a surprise, sweetie, but I think it's time you knew—Zach's your daddy."

Rowdy looked from his mother to Zach, surprise making a round O of his cherub mouth. He blinked and eyed Zach. "You're my daddy? Really?"

"Yeah, really." Zach met the little boy's stare with serious consideration. "What do you think?"

Both adults held their breaths.

Then Rowdy threw himself off Jessie's lap and onto Zach's. "Wow, this is great! Wait till I tell Cody that I have a new dad! Does this mean I get to have all the puppies? How about a horse? Cody's daddy gave him a pony and he said if I had a daddy I'd probably have a pony, too."

Zach's stunned gaze met Jessie's over the top of Rowdy's head, relief mixed with sheer joy. Then he stood, swinging Rowdy into the air and holding him suspended above his head.

"Yes, you can have all the puppies but your mom and I will have to talk about the pony."

"Yay!"

Jessie watched the two males, big and small, as Zach pretended to let Rowdy wrestle him to the floor and climb on top of him. The little boy talked nonstop.

Rowdy's temperature was nearly normal but Jessie, worried about a relapse, kept the rest of the day quiet. Zach secured a loose board on the garden shed in Jessie's backyard, aided by Rowdy wielding a small hammer. The adults sat patiently through thirty minutes of Rowdy's favorite Elmo video after dinner before tucking him in bed.

"Will you be here when I wake up in the morning?" Rowdy asked Zach.

"Not tomorrow. I have to start work early in the morning, long before you wake up."

"What are you doing?"

"Rounding up cattle," Zach replied. "But maybe your mom can drive you out to visit tomorrow night."

"Can we, Mommy?"

"We'll see," Jessie said diplomatically. "It depends on how you feel tomorrow and whether you still have a fever."

"So you'd better get lots of rest tonight," Zach told him.

"'Kay." He squeezed his eyes shut and they left the room.

"Isn't Charlie out of town?" Jessie asked when they reached the living room.

"He is." Zach reached for her, pulling her close as he walked to the door. "Which means I've got a long day ahead of me."

"You aren't chasing cattle in by yourself, are you?"

"Yup, just me. It'll take longer, but I don't have a choice. I've put it off longer than I'd planned." He bent his head, nuzzling her throat and the soft skin above the neck of her shirt. "Damn, I love the way you smell. What is that?"

She laughed, his hair tickling the underside of her chin. "It's a perfume my mom brought me from Paris."

"It makes me want to lick you all over."

"Oh." She tried unsuccessfully to wipe that image from her mind. Then he lifted his head, his eyes hot, and he kissed her, smoothing his hand down her back to press her closer before cupping her bottom and lifting her into him.

When he finally took his mouth from hers, they were both breathless and if he hadn't been holding her, she would have slid right to the floor.

"I have to go home," he muttered, his lips brushing the curve of her ear.

"Why?" she murmured, distracted. "Oh, that's right. You have to work tomorrow."

"Yeah. And I have to check on Zarina and the pups. I called Rachel on my way to the hospital last night and asked her to check on the dogs and horses this morning. But I have evening chores to do before I can go to bed tonight." He kissed her temples, and the curve of her cheek before he took her mouth again. Long moments passed before his arms reluctantly loosened. "I wish I didn't have to leave."

"It's probably for the best," she said. "The Harrises will certainly notice if your truck is parked outside my door for a second night in a row. Last night I can explain because Rowdy was ill, but I don't want them thinking we're living in sin."

"Marry me and we'll be legal."

"I'll think about it," she murmured.

"Don't take too long."

"What time do you have to be awake in the morning?" she asked, changing the subject.

"Before the sun comes up." He released her and threaded his fingers through hers. "You're sure Rowdy will be okay?"

"Yes. He's had ear infections before and I can

tell the antibiotic is doing its job. He's much better. If the drug wasn't working, he'd still be running a temperature and be lethargic."

Zach nodded and carried her fingers to his lips, pressing a kiss in her palm. "I have to go."

Jessie stood on the porch, watching until his taillights disappeared when he turned at the end of the block.

She doubted they'd see him for a few days. Without help, it was likely to take more than tomorrow to gather a herd of cattle scattered over who knew how many acres.

Unless... She stopped, considering an idea, then picked up the phone.

Chapter Nine

Zach rose before dawn. The herd of cattle he needed to bring in was fairly small but the animals were likely to be scattered over several hundred acres of pasture. He left the house, carrying a water bottle and sandwiches, and crossed the dark barnyard, rolling back the heavy barn door and entering the dim interior. His quarter horse, General Patton, stretched his neck over the top of the stall gate and whickered.

"Hey, boy." Zach paused to rub the General's

nose. "Are you ready to stop lazing around this comfortable stall and get to work?"

The horse's ears flicked forward and he turned his head to follow Zach's progress as he walked to the grain bin, filled a can with oats and returned with it to the General's stall. Zach left the Appaloosa crunching the feed and checked on Zarina and her pups, filling her water dish and food bowl, before he carried a saddle, bridle and the rest of the horse's gear from the tack room.

Zach had just finished saddling the General and led him from the stall when the rumble of an engine sounded outside, growing louder.

"What the hell?" Zach saw the arc of headlights outside the open barn door and then heard the engine switch off.

A vehicle door slammed.

"Zach?" Jessie's voice called. Seconds later, she appeared in the doorway and entered the barn. "Hey." She smiled, walking quickly toward him. "I hoped I'd catch you before you left."

"Hey, yourself. What are you doing here?"

"I trailered my horse over. I'm going to help you round up cattle today." She reached him and looped her arms around his neck, going up on tip-toe to kiss him.

Zach caught her around the waist and deepened the kiss, wishing they weren't both wearing jackets. At last he let her go and she stepped back, hair mussed, eyes dark.

"Where's Rowdy?" he asked.

"Mom's watching him today. She's getting in some quality Grandma-time." She slipped her arm through his and walked beside him as he led the General through the wide doorway. "I haven't done this in ages. It's going to be fun."

"Fun?" He shook his head. "You think heat, dust and a sore butt from riding all day sounds like fun?"

"Absolutely. But I prefer to think of it as spending a sunny day in the fresh air, on horseback, getting lots of healthy exercise."

"You're an optimist but I can use the help so I'm not about to disillusion you. The minute you get tired, though, I'm sending you back to the house." He tied the rangy Appaloosa to a corral post and headed to the back of Jessie's horse trailer.

They unloaded her horse and Jessie took the mare's reins while Zach slammed the end-gate shut. The growl of truck engines broke the hush of dawn once more and he turned to look down the gravel ranch road. Three sets of headlights turned off the highway and moved slowly toward them down the lane, all of the vehicles pulling horse trailers.

"What's going on?" Zach looked at Jessie but she shook her head, baffled.

The pickup trucks parked in the wide expanse of graveled yard between the house and barn. John McCloud stepped out of the first truck, Luke and Rachel from the second and Chase left the third.

Zach had no clue what they were doing here and without conscious thought, stepped to the left and slightly in front of Jessie, putting himself between her and the three big men.

"Oh, for heaven's sake, Zach, stop it." Jessie's voice was low and probably only he could hear, but he had no doubt she was annoyed with him. "Hi, Dad." She lifted her voice from murmur to clear greeting. "What brings you out so early in the morning?"

Luke and Chase joined their father, one on each side with Rachel on her husband's left. She winked at Jessie and smiled. Zach still didn't know what was going on, but his internal radar switched off and his tension eased a fraction.

"Mornin', Jessie." John McCloud's voice held no underlying currents that Zach could detect. In fact, he sounded downright friendly. "Your mother told us you were helping Zach chase cattle this morning. We didn't have anything better to do, so we thought we'd join you." He looked at Zach. "That is, if you don't mind the company, son."

Son? Zach was stunned. If he were seated, he'd have fallen off his chair. Instead, he merely nodded. "I'd appreciate the help, Mr. McCloud."

"Me and the boys will unload the horses." John jerked his thumb toward the trailers. "Won't take but a few minutes."

The three men walked to the trailers while Rachel joined Zach and Jessie.

"What's going on, Rach?" Zach asked. The noise of clanging gates and rattle of horses' hooves on metal and wood made it impossible for anyone but his sister and Jessie to hear his question.

"I told Luke you were rounding up cattle today and I planned to join you since Charlie couldn't be here." Rachel gestured at the activity by the trailers. "He got up when I did this morning and said he thought he'd come along and keep me company."

"Really?" Jessie's eyebrows lifted in surprise. "That's all he said?"

"Yes. No explanation as to why he's helping us—and when I asked him, he'd only tell me it seemed like a good day to go riding."

"Huh." Zach looked at Jessie. "That's the same reason you gave—did you ask Luke to help?"

"No," Jessie said firmly. "And I wouldn't. I didn't say anything to Dad or Chase, either. Mom must have mentioned why she's babysitting Rowdy today and they came up with this on their own."

"Interesting that they all decided to go riding on the same day," Rachel commented.

"I hope it means more than that," Jessie said, eyeing her father and brothers as they slammed the last trailer gate shut and led their horses forward.

"I wouldn't count on it. It probably doesn't mean anything more than Luke helping Rachel and your dad and Chase helping you," Zach commented.

"I hope you're wrong." Jessie didn't sound convinced of it, though.

Zach decided he was thankful for their help and wouldn't look for underlying reasons.

"How do you want to do this, Zach?" Jessie's dad asked.

"I'd planned to start in the farthest corner of the south pasture. That section is the roughest land with breaks and scrub brush. It'll be the hardest riding."

John nodded. "Best to get the worst done early while everybody's fresh. You're going to run the herd in this morning and brand this afternoon?"

"That's my plan. They need to be inoculated, too."

"Sounds good," John agreed. "Chase and me are used to working together so if it's all the same to you, we'll ride together."

Zach nodded and without further comment, John mounted his horse. Chase followed suit and Luke handed Rachel the reins to a sorrel gelding, giving her a leg up before he settled into the saddle of a compact bay quarter horse.

Jessie swung aboard her mare and Zach mounted the General, leading the way out of the ranch yard. The McClouds followed, the six riders strung out two by two as the sun edged above the horizon, chasing away the shadows and gilding horses and riders with pale gold.

The morning was hot and dusty but with six seasoned riders instead of Zach on his own, the cattle were gathered with a minimum of complications. When they drove the small herd into the ranch yard just after noon, Jessie had new freckles across the bridge of her nose from the sun's rays and sweat dampened the back of her T-shirt. All of them had stripped off their jackets and tied them behind their saddles as the day grew hotter.

A dark green SUV was parked next to the McCloud pickup trucks. Margaret McCloud stood in the bed of her husband's truck, restraining Rowdy with a grip on the waist of his jeans. He jumped up and down beside her, waving and shouting as the cattle streamed past the pickup, funneling through the open gates to the pens beyond the corral and barn.

Once the cattle were penned in, the riders joined the excited Rowdy at the truck, while Zach leaned out of his saddle and closed the gate on the last straggler.

"Uncle Chase! Uncle Chase!" Rowdy called.

Zach looked over his shoulder. Jessie and the rest of the McClouds had surrounded the truck bed and Rowdy was holding his arms out to Chase.

He watched Jessie's brother swing Rowdy from the truck bed, seating him on the saddle in front of him. The dark-haired little boy beamed and said something that Zach couldn't hear, but that made all the adults around him laugh. Jessie looked over her shoulder and beckoned. Reluctant though he was to join what was clearly a family gathering, Zach lifted the reins and kneed the big Appaloosa into a walk.

"Mom brought lunch, Zach," Jessie called as he neared them.

Rowdy wriggled in Chase's hold, his eyes

lighting. "Zach's here. Let me go, Uncle Chase. I wanna ride with Daddy."

Zach felt his little boy's words like a punch to the heart. His hand tightened unconsciously on the reins, bringing the well-trained General to a halt.

The adults were silent, the air suddenly thick with tension.

Rowdy was oblivious to the emotion charging the atmosphere. He tugged at Chase's arm and frowned up at him. "Uncle Chase? Did you hear me? I wanna go ride with my daddy."

Chase's features seemed carved in stone as he stared at Zach but then he looked down at Rowdy. "You do, huh?"

Chase guided his quarter horse toward Zach, distancing himself from the cluster of silently watching riders by the truck, out of hearing range.

"The kid wants to ride with you." He lifted Rowdy free of the saddle, his legs dangling, and handed him to Zach, who tucked him safely in front of him. "I'm assuming you and my sister will be seeing a minister soon." It wasn't a question. In fact, Chase's calm demand was far closer to a statement of intent.

"I've already asked her," Zach replied, his voice carrying the same level of warning. To his surprise, a brief smile lit Chase's eyes.

"That doesn't mean she'll say yes. I suggest you tie her up and kidnap her."

"Thanks for the advice," Zach said, half grinning at the prospect.

Chase nodded abruptly and turned away. "Hey, Mom," he said over his shoulder. "Is that barbecue beef I smell?"

The spell was broken. In the ensuing stir of dismounting, unsaddling horses and eating lunch, Zach didn't have a moment alone with Jessie. They didn't have time to talk until much later, after the McCloud clan had left for home and he followed Jessie back into town to share Rowdy's bedtime ritual of bath and the reading of several Sandra Boynton stories. Finally, Rowdy was tucked in for the night.

In the hall outside his bedroom, Zach took Jessie's hand and tugged her toward her room.

"At last, I've got you alone." He wrapped his arms around her and kissed her, tumbling them both onto the soft mattress of her bed.

Jessie reveled in the heavy press of his body, the heat of his mouth on hers and the slow stroke of his hand on the skin of her midriff beneath her rucked-up T-shirt. She was nearly dizzy with desire when he lifted his mouth and braced himself on his elbows, his hands in her hair and looked down at her.

"What is it?"

"Today your brother Chase and the rest of your family pretty much gave their approval. You've had twenty-four hours to think about getting married. I need an answer."

She stared at him, unable to answer. Could she marry him when he didn't love her? Was great sex—no, actually, it was fantastic sex—enough to make a marriage work when only one of them was in love?

"I'm not sure we can make a marriage last without love, Zach."

His eyelids lowered and she caught the flash of pain in his eyes.

"I know you think great sex and sharing a child is enough to keep us together, Zach, but I just don't know if it will. And if and when I marry, I need to know there's love on both sides." Her voice broke, tears threatening.

"You don't think it's possible you could grow to love me?" His voice was gravelly.

"I already do love you," she said, swiping at the tears with frustration. "That's not the point. I think we should go on as we are and see how things develop."

He caught her hands and held them still, glaring at her. "What do you mean, that's not the point? If you love me and I love you, then I don't see the problem."

"You love me?"

"Yes, damn it, I love you. And for the record, I don't want to go on as we are. I want to marry you. I want us living together permanently with Rowdy sleeping down the hall and you in my bed every night."

"You do?" she repeated, dumbstruck by the heat of annoyance and arousal in his eyes.

"Yes, I do. Now say yes."

"Yes." She smiled at him, charmed.

"Thank God." His lips hovered just above hers,

his eyes narrowing over her. "Are you always going to be this cooperative?'

"No."

"Good. I'd hate to be bored." And he took her mouth while one hand shoved her T-shirt higher to cup her breast in an act of pure possession.

That will certainly never happen, Jessie thought blissfully, tugging at his shirt.

* * * * *

Watch for the next book in Lois Faye Dyer's
THE McCLOUDS OF MONTANA *miniseries,*
CHASE'S PROMISE
Coming November 2006 only from
Silhouette Special Edition.

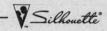

SPECIAL EDITION™

COMING IN SEPTEMBER FROM
USA TODAY BESTSELLING AUTHOR

SUSAN MALLERY

THE LADIES' MAN

Rachel Harper wondered how she'd tell
Carter Brockett the news—their spontaneous
night of passion had left her pregnant!
What would he think of the naive
schoolteacher who'd lost control? After
all, the man had a legion of exes who'd
been unable to snare a commitment, and
here she had a forever-binding one!

Then she remembered.
He'd lost control, too....

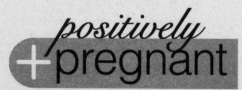

positively
+*pregnant*

**Sometimes the unexpected
is the best news of all...**

Visit Silhouette Books at www.eHarlequin.com   SSETLM

SAVE UP TO $30! SIGN UP TODAY!

INSIDE *Romance*

The complete guide to your favorite
Harlequin®, Silhouette® and Love Inspired® books.

✓ Newsletter ABSOLUTELY FREE! No purchase necessary.

✓ Valuable coupons for future purchases of Harlequin,
  Silhouette and Love Inspired books in every issue!

✓ Special excerpts & previews in each issue. Learn about all
  the hottest titles before they arrive in stores.

✓ No hassle—mailed directly to your door!

✓ Comes complete with a handy shopping checklist
  so you won't miss out on any titles.

- -

SIGN ME UP TO RECEIVE INSIDE ROMANCE
ABSOLUTELY FREE
(Please print clearly)

Name

Address

City/Town   State/Province   Zip/Postal Code

(098 KKM EJL9)

Please mail this form to:
In the U.S.A.: Inside Romance, P.O. Box 9057, Buffalo, NY 14269-9057
In Canada: Inside Romance, P.O. Box 622, Fort Erie, ON L2A 5X3
OR visit http://www.eHarlequin.com/insideromance

IRNBPA06R   ® and ™ are trademarks owned and used by the trademark owner and/or its licensee.

Silhouette® Desire.®

**Introducing an exciting appearance
by legendary
New York Times bestselling author**

DIANA PALMER

HEARTBREAKER

He's the ultimate bachelor...
but he may have just met
the one woman to change his ways!

Join the drama in the story of a confirmed
bachelor, an amnesiac beauty and their
unexpected passionate romance.

**"Diana Palmer is a mesmerizing storyteller
who captures the essence of what
a romance should be."—*Affaire de Coeur***

**Heartbreaker *is available from Silhouette Desire
in September 2006.***

Visit Silhouette Books at www.eHarlequin.com SDDPIBC

If you enjoyed what you just read,
then we've got an offer you can't resist!

Take 2 bestselling
love stories FREE!
Plus get a FREE surprise gift!

Clip this page and mail it to Silhouette Reader Service™

IN U.S.A.
3010 Walden Ave.
P.O. Box 1867
Buffalo, N.Y. 14240-1867

IN CANADA
P.O. Box 609
Fort Erie, Ontario
L2A 5X3

YES! Please send me 2 free Silhouette Special Edition® novels and my free surprise gift. After receiving them, if I don't wish to receive anymore, I can return the shipping statement marked cancel. If I don't cancel, I will receive 6 brand-new novels every month, before they're available in stores! In the U.S.A., bill me at the bargain price of $4.24 plus 25¢ shipping and handling per book and applicable sales tax, if any*. In Canada, bill me at the bargain price of $4.99 plus 25¢ shipping and handling per book and applicable taxes**. That's the complete price and a savings of at least 10% off the cover prices—what a great deal! I understand that accepting the 2 free books and gift places me under no obligation ever to buy any books. I can always return a shipment and cancel at any time. Even if I never buy another book from Silhouette, the 2 free books and gift are mine to keep forever.

235 SDN DZ9D
335 SDN DZ9E

Name	(PLEASE PRINT)	
Address	Apt.#	
City	State/Prov.	Zip/Postal Code

Not valid to current Silhouette Special Edition® subscribers.

Want to try two free books from another series?
Call 1-800-873-8635 or visit www.morefreebooks.com.

* Terms and prices subject to change without notice. Sales tax applicable in N.Y.
** Canadian residents will be charged applicable provincial taxes and GST.
   All orders subject to approval. Offer limited to one per household.
   ® are registered trademarks owned and used by the trademark owner and or its licensee.

SPED04R   ©2004 Harlequin Enterprises Limited

The first novel in the new
Lakeshore Chronicles from
New York Times bestselling author

SUSAN WIGGS

Real estate expert Olivia Bellamy
reluctantly trades a trendy Manhattan
summer for her family's old resort
camp in the Catskills, where her
primary task will be renovating
the bungalow colony for her
grandparents, who want one last
summer together filled with fun,
friends and family. A posh resort in its
heyday, the camp is now in disarray,
and Olivia is forced to hire contractor
Connor Davis—a still-smoldering
flame from her own summers at camp.
But as the days grow warm, not even
the inviting blue waters of Willow
Lake can cool the passions flaring or
keep shocking secrets at bay.

Summer
at Willow Lake

"...another excellent title to her
already outstanding body of work."
—*Booklist (starred review)* on Table For Five

*Available the first week of August 2006,
wherever paperbacks are sold!*

MIRA®

www.MIRABooks.com

MSW2325

HARLEQUIN® *Blaze*

"Super-steamy!"
—*Cosmopolitan* magazine

New York Times bestselling author

Elizabeth Bevarly

delivers another sexy adventure!

As a former vice cop, small-town police chief
Sam Maguire knows when things don't add up.
And there's definitely something suspicious happen-
ing behind the scenes at Rosie Bliss's flower shop.
Rumor has it she's not selling just flowers.
But once he gets close and gets his hands on her,
uh, goods, he's in big trouble…of the sensual kind!

Pick up your copy of

MY ONLY VICE

by Elizabeth Bevarly

*Available this September,
wherever series romances are sold.*

www.eHarlequin.com

HBEB0906

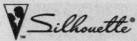

COMING NEXT MONTH

SPECIAL EDITION

#1777 MARRIED IN HASTE—Christine Rimmer
Bravo Family Ties
When it came to grand fiery passions, Angie Dellazola had been there, done that—and been burned. Marrying steady-minded hometown boy Brett Bravo seemed like the ticket to the quiet life…until pent-up passions exploded between the unsuspecting newlyweds!

#1778 THE LADIES' MAN—Susan Mallery
Positively Pregnant
Rachel Harper wasn't the one-night-stand type, but when sexy Carter Brockett offered the stranded kindergarten teacher a ride, one thing led to another…. And now Rachel had news for the ladies' man—she was pregnant….

#1779 EXPECTING HIS BROTHER'S BABY—
Karen Rose Smith
Baby Bonds
When Brock Warner returned to Saddle Ridge, he found the family ranch falling to pieces, its custodian—his pregnant, recently widowed sister-in-law, Kylie Armstrong Warner— in the hospital, and his own long-buried feelings for her resurfacing in a big way….

#1780 A LITTLE CHANGE OF PLANS—Jen Safrey
Talk of the Neighborhood
Pregnant after a college reunion fling, consultant Molly Jackson's business and reputation were on the line. So she turned to her laid-back best friend Adam Shibbs for a cover-up marriage of convenience—but would real love spring from their short-term charade?

#1781 UNDER THE WESTERN SKY—Laurie Paige
Canyon Country
When mild-mannered midwife Julianne Martin was accused of trafficking stolen Native American artifacts, Park Service investigator Tony Aquilon realized he had the wrong woman…or did he?

#1782 THE RIGHT BROTHER—Patricia McLinn
Seasons in a Small Town
A deadbeat ex had left Jennifer Truesdale and her daughter high and dry—until her ex's brother, Trent Stenner, saved the day, buying out the family car dealership and giving Jennifer a job. But was the former football pro just making a pass at this lady in distress?

SSECNM0806